W9-CFV-094

Barbie™

Big Dreams, Best Friends

PAPERCUT**Z**™

NEW YORK

#2 "Big Dreams, Best Friends"

SARAH KUHN – Writer
YISHAN LI – Artist
ALITHA MARTINEZ – Cover
LAURIE E. SMITH – Colorist
JANICE CHIANG – Letterer

DAWN GUZZO – Production Coordinator
MARIAH MCCOURT – Editor
JEFF WHITMAN – Assistant Managing Editor
JIM SALICRUP
Editor-in-Chief

Special thanks to Bethany Bryan and Beth Scorzato

ISBN: 978-1-62991-616-3 paperback edition
ISBN: 978-1-62991-617-0 hardcover edition

Papercutz books may be purchased for business or
promotional use. For information on bulk purchases please
contact Macmillan Corporate and Premium Sales
Department at (800) 221-7945 x5442.

Printed in China
July 2017

Distributed by Macmillan
First Printing

DOES SHE LIKE IT, WHITNEY?
BARBIE, SHHH...
WHAT IF SHE DOESN'T LIKE IT?
SHE'LL LIKE IT.
HOW DO YOU KNOW?
I JUST DO.
BUT...
I DON'T LIKE IT!

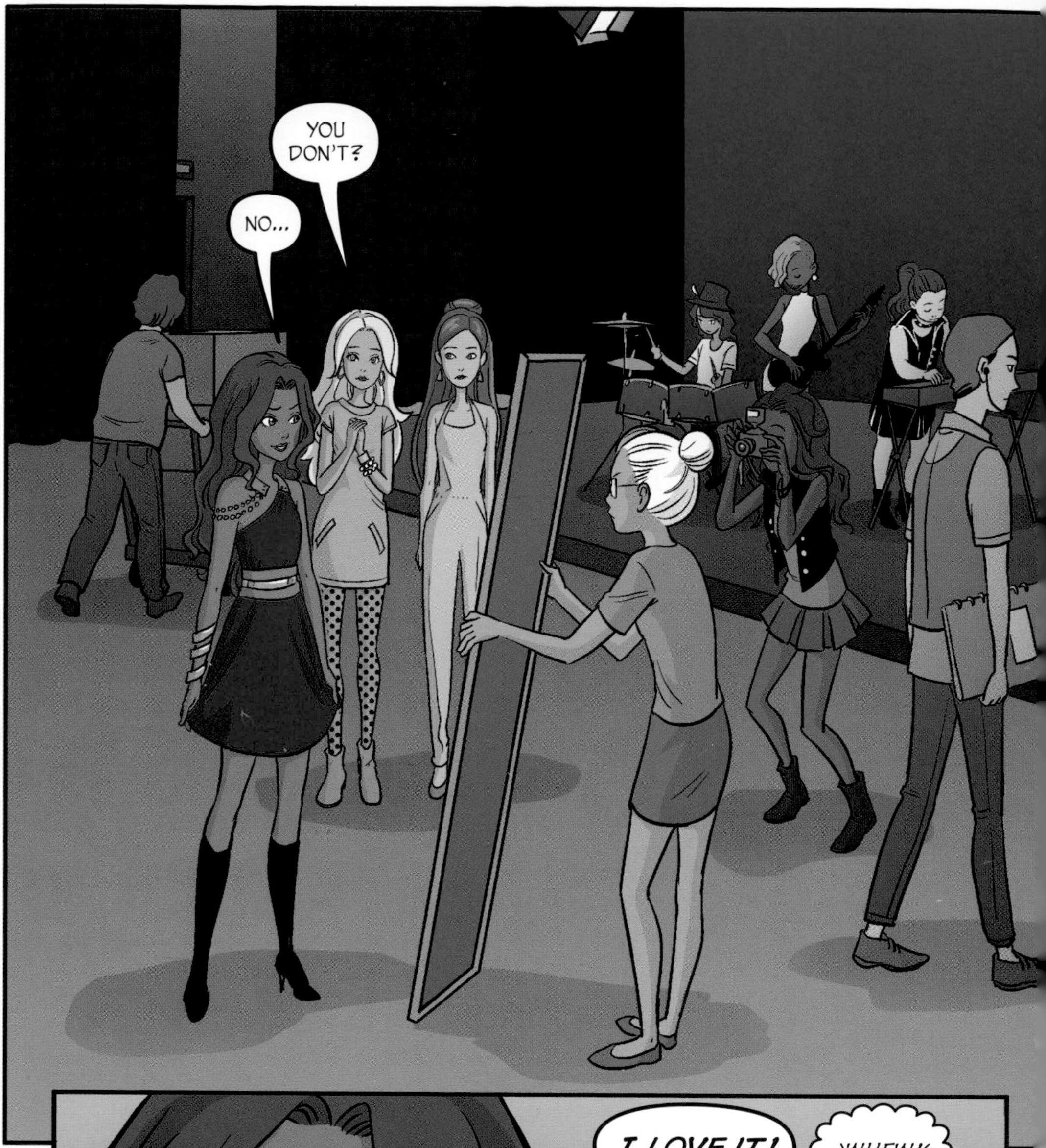
NO...
YOU DON'T?

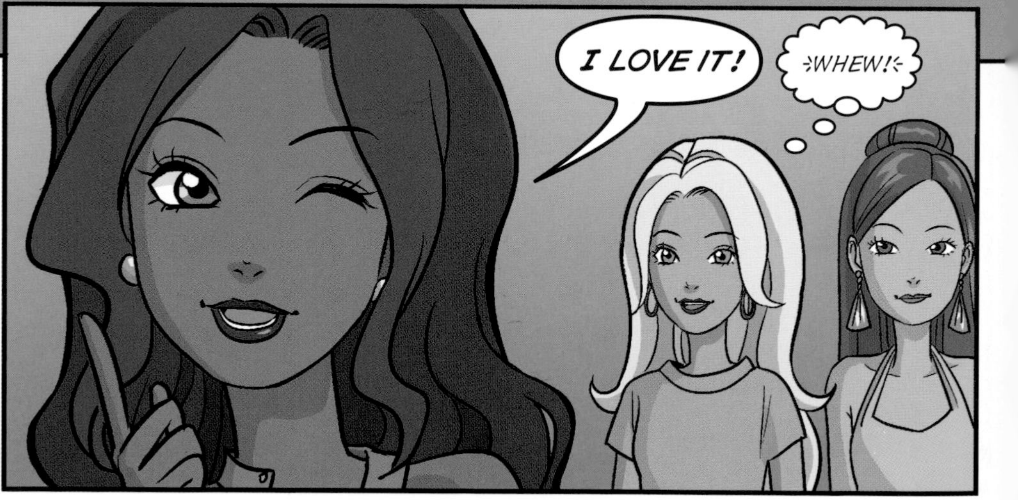
I LOVE IT!
WHEW!

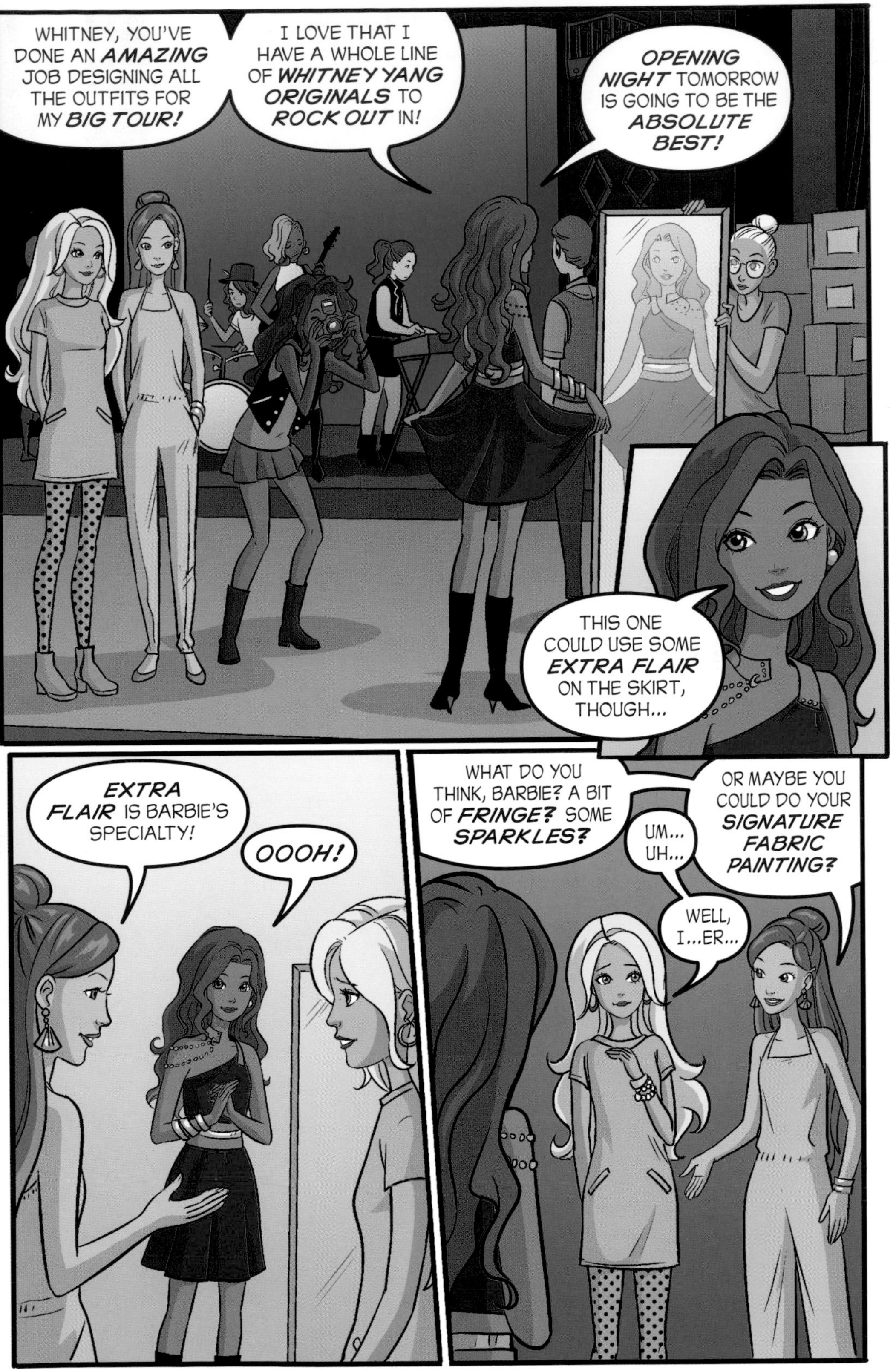
WHITNEY, YOU'VE DONE AN AMAZING JOB DESIGNING ALL THE OUTFITS FOR MY BIG TOUR!
I LOVE THAT I HAVE A WHOLE LINE OF WHITNEY YANG ORIGINALS TO ROCK OUT IN!
OPENING NIGHT TOMORROW IS GOING TO BE THE ABSOLUTE BEST!
THIS ONE COULD USE SOME EXTRA FLAIR ON THE SKIRT, THOUGH...
EXTRA FLAIR IS BARBIE'S SPECIALTY!
OOOH!
WHAT DO YOU THINK, BARBIE? A BIT OF FRINGE? SOME SPARKLES?
UM... UH...
OR MAYBE YOU COULD DO YOUR SIGNATURE FABRIC PAINTING?
WELL, I...ER...

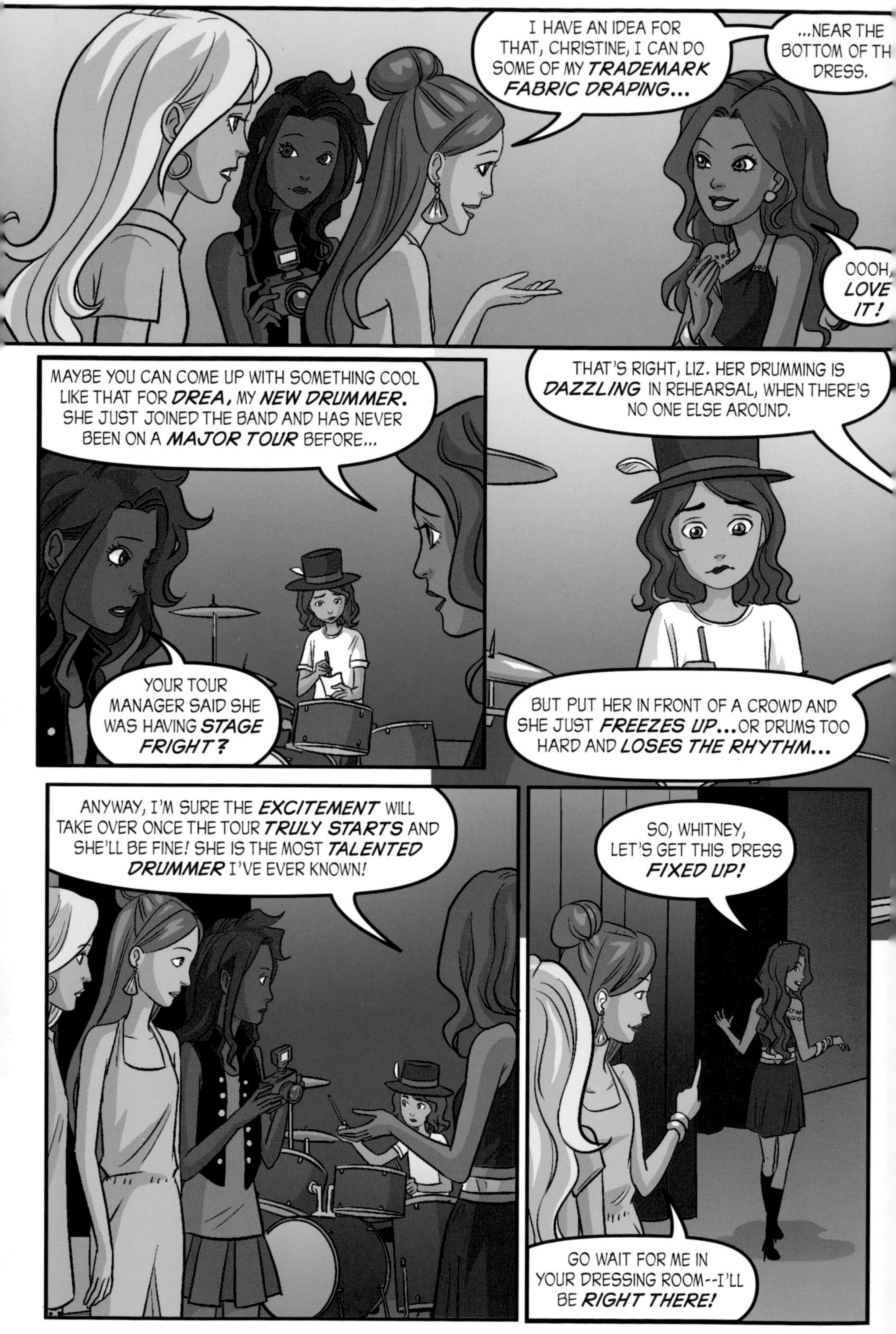
I HAVE AN IDEA FOR THAT, CHRISTINE, I CAN DO SOME OF MY TRADEMARK FABRIC DRAPING...
...NEAR THE BOTTOM OF TH DRESS.
OOOH, LOVE IT!
MAYBE YOU CAN COME UP WITH SOMETHING COOL LIKE THAT FOR DREA, MY NEW DRUMMER. SHE JUST JOINED THE BAND AND HAS NEVER BEEN ON A MAJOR TOUR BEFORE...
YOUR TOUR MANAGER SAID SHE WAS HAVING STAGE FRIGHT?
THAT'S RIGHT, LIZ. HER DRUMMING IS DAZZLING IN REHEARSAL, WHEN THERE'S NO ONE ELSE AROUND.
BUT PUT HER IN FRONT OF A CROWD AND SHE JUST FREEZES UP...OR DRUMS TOO HARD AND LOSES THE RHYTHM...
ANYWAY, I'M SURE THE EXCITEMENT WILL TAKE OVER ONCE THE TOUR TRULY STARTS AND SHE'LL BE FINE! SHE IS THE MOST TALENTED DRUMMER I'VE EVER KNOWN!
SO, WHITNEY, LET'S GET THIS DRESS FIXED UP!
GO WAIT FOR ME IN YOUR DRESSING ROOM--I'LL BE RIGHT THERE!

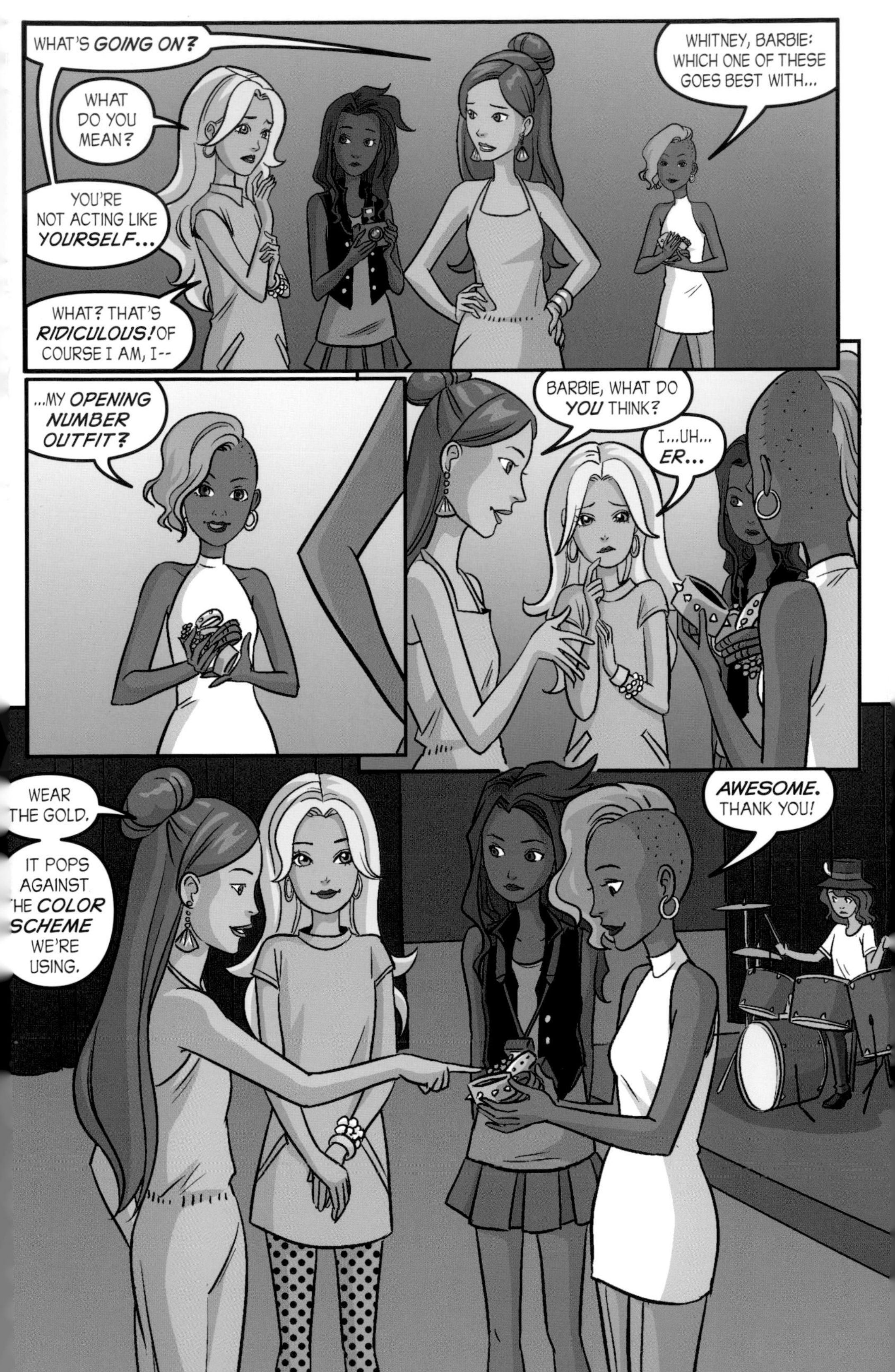
WHAT'S GOING ON?
WHAT DO YOU MEAN?
YOU'RE NOT ACTING LIKE YOURSELF...
WHAT? THAT'S RIDICULOUS! OF COURSE I AM, I--
WHITNEY, BARBIE: WHICH ONE OF THESE GOES BEST WITH...
...MY OPENING NUMBER OUTFIT?
BARBIE, WHAT DO YOU THINK?
I...UH... ER...
WEAR THE GOLD.
IT POPS AGAINST THE COLOR SCHEME WE'RE USING.
AWESOME. THANK YOU!

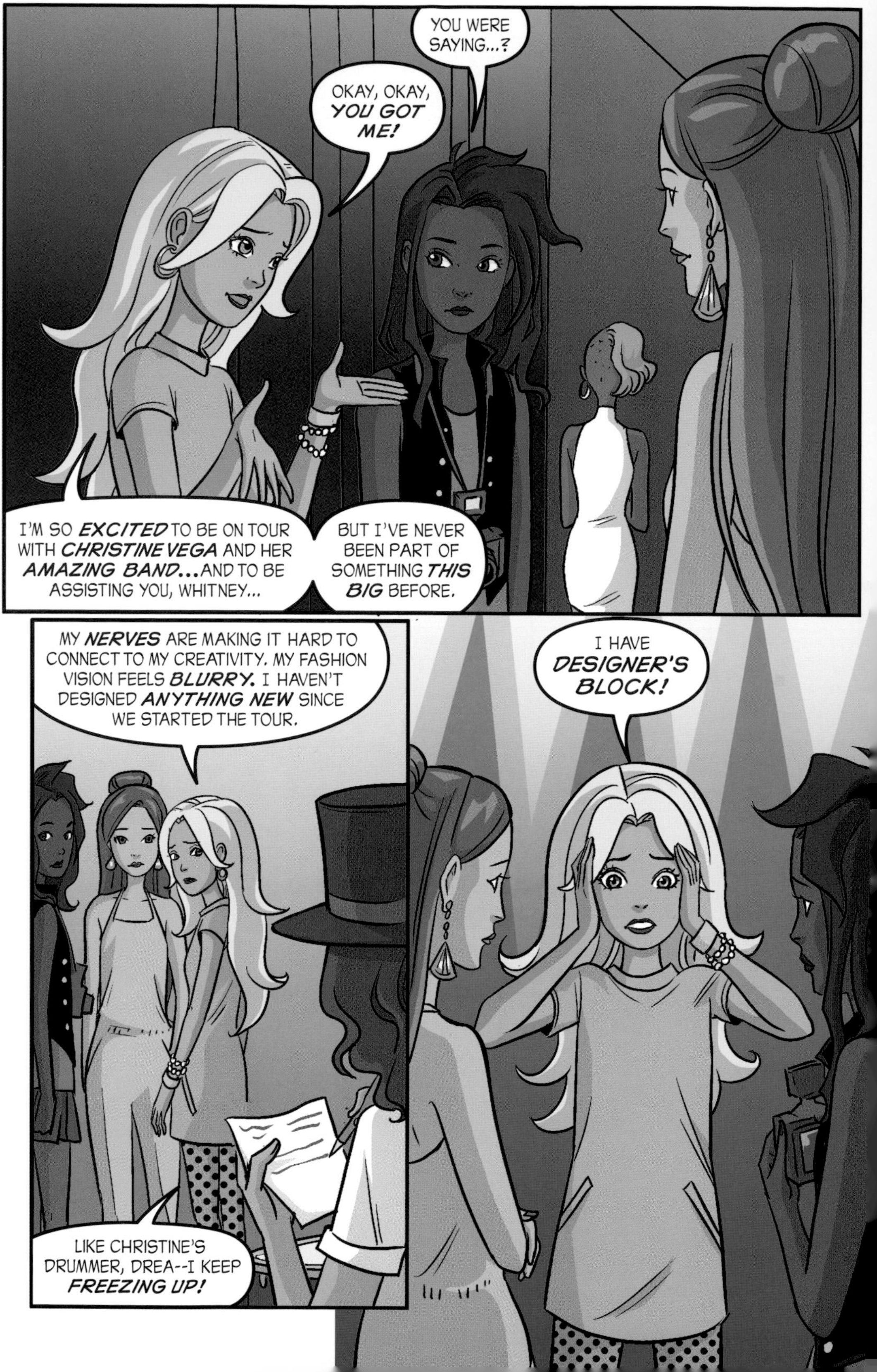
YOU WERE SAYING...?
OKAY, OKAY, YOU GOT ME!
I'M SO EXCITED TO BE ON TOUR WITH CHRISTINE VEGA AND HER AMAZING BAND...AND TO BE ASSISTING YOU, WHITNEY...
BUT I'VE NEVER BEEN PART OF SOMETHING THIS BIG BEFORE.
MY NERVES ARE MAKING IT HARD TO CONNECT TO MY CREATIVITY. MY FASHION VISION FEELS BLURRY. I HAVEN'T DESIGNED ANYTHING NEW SINCE WE STARTED THE TOUR.
LIKE CHRISTINE'S DRUMMER, DREA--I KEEP FREEZING UP!
I HAVE DESIGNER'S BLOCK!

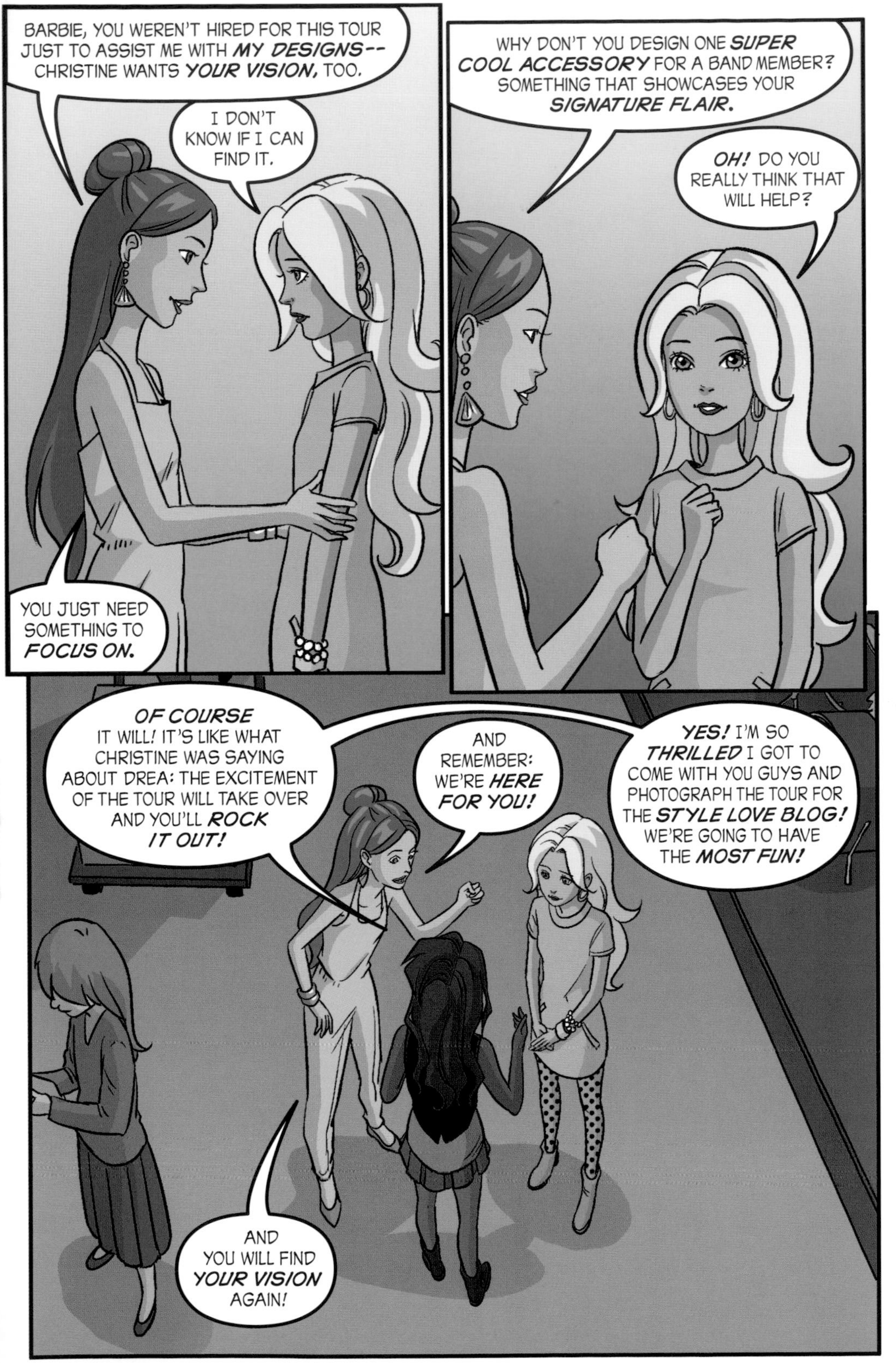

BARBIE, YOU WEREN'T HIRED FOR THIS TOUR JUST TO ASSIST ME WITH MY DESIGNS-- CHRISTINE WANTS YOUR VISION, TOO.
I DON'T KNOW IF I CAN FIND IT.
YOU JUST NEED SOMETHING TO FOCUS ON.
WHY DON'T YOU DESIGN ONE SUPER COOL ACCESSORY FOR A BAND MEMBER? SOMETHING THAT SHOWCASES YOUR SIGNATURE FLAIR.
OH! DO YOU REALLY THINK THAT WILL HELP?
OF COURSE IT WILL! IT'S LIKE WHAT CHRISTINE WAS SAYING ABOUT DREA: THE EXCITEMENT OF THE TOUR WILL TAKE OVER AND YOU'LL ROCK IT OUT!
AND YOU WILL FIND YOUR VISION AGAIN!
AND REMEMBER: WE'RE HERE FOR YOU!
YES! I'M SO THRILLED I GOT TO COME WITH YOU GUYS AND PHOTOGRAPH THE TOUR FOR THE STYLE LOVE BLOG! WE'RE GOING TO HAVE THE MOST FUN!

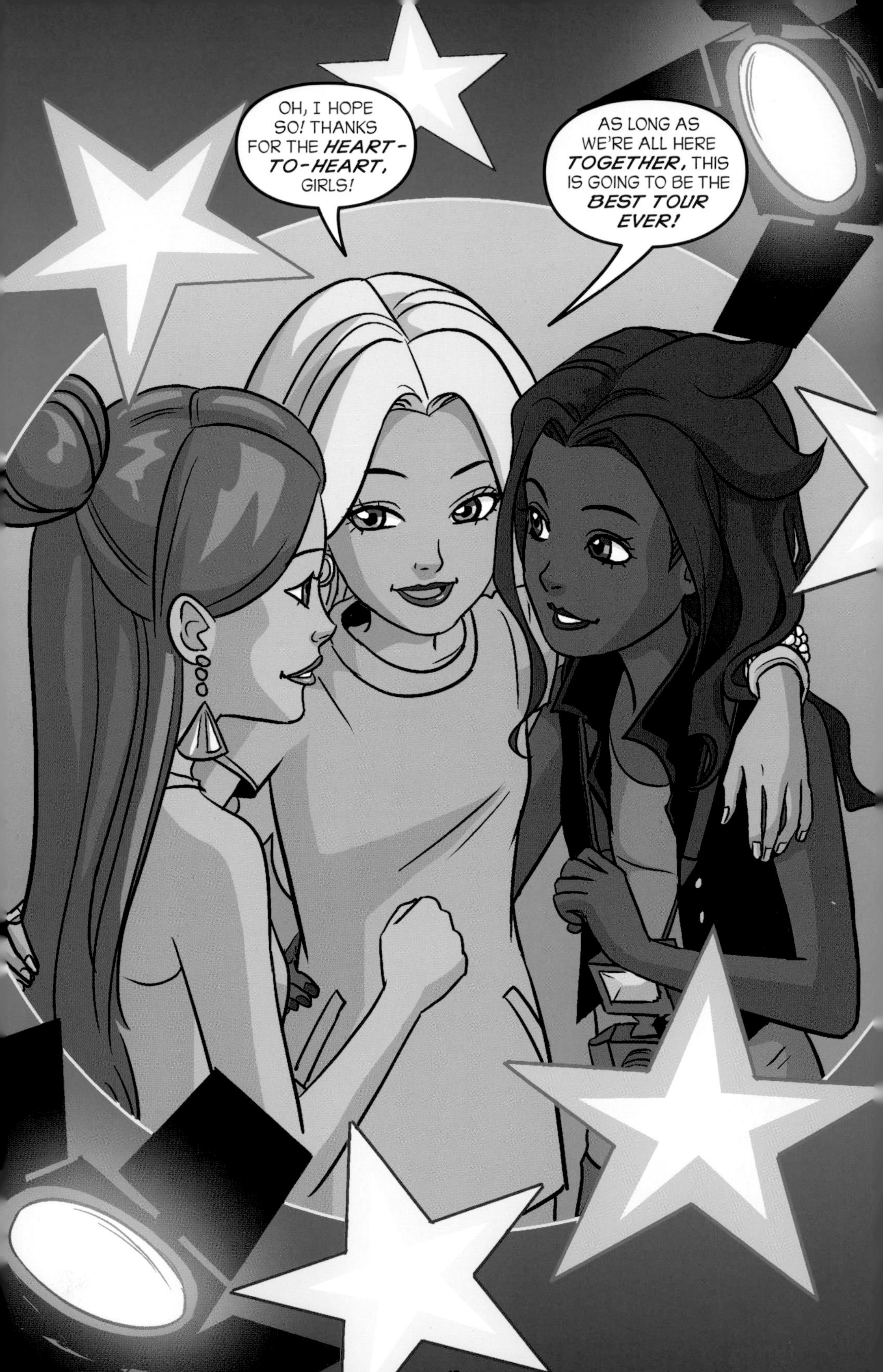
OH, I HOPE SO! THANKS FOR THE HEART-TO-HEART, GIRLS!
AS LONG AS WE'RE ALL HERE TOGETHER, THIS IS GOING TO BE THE BEST TOUR EVER!

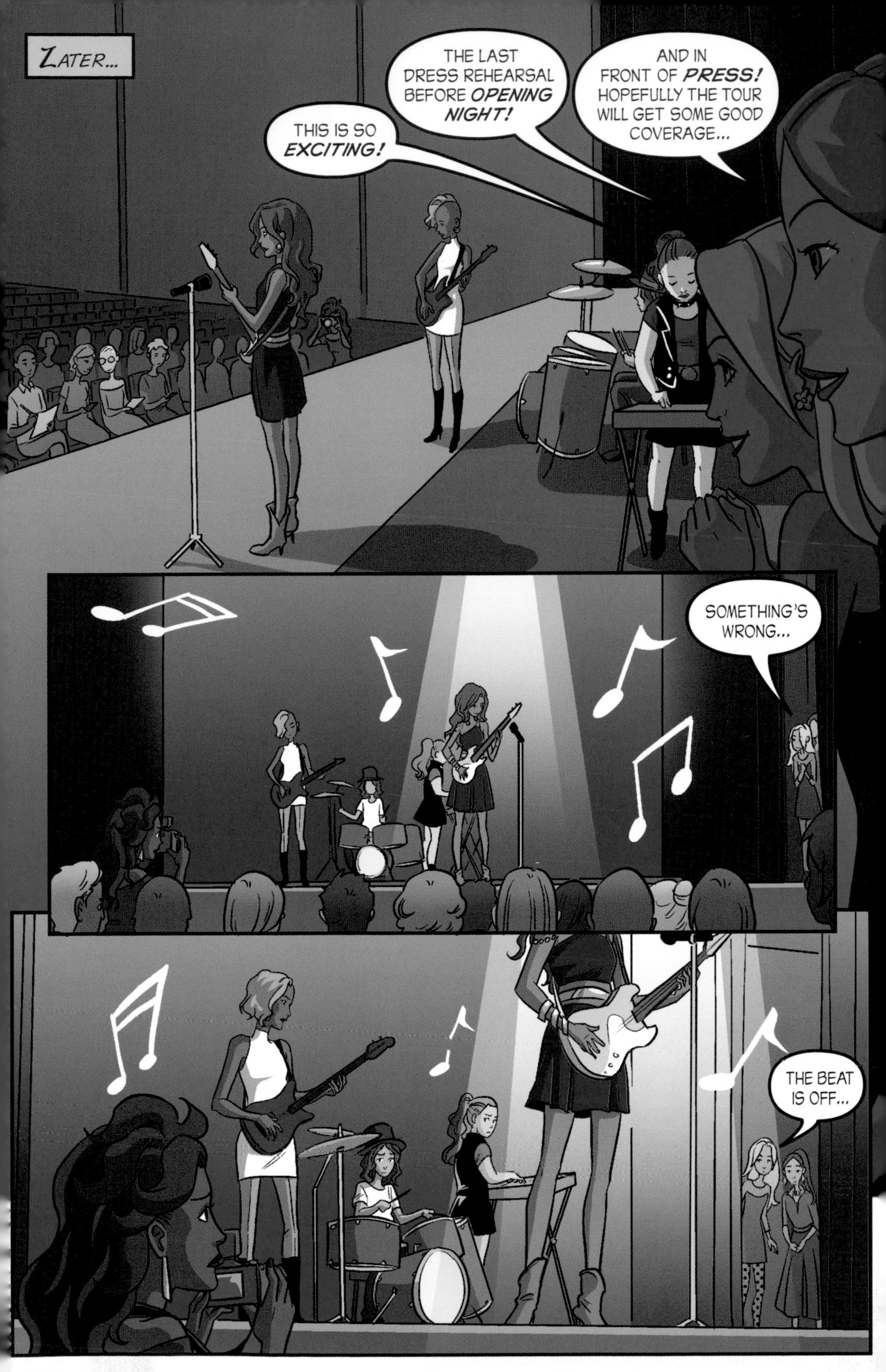
LATER...
THIS IS SO EXCITING!
THE LAST DRESS REHEARSAL BEFORE OPENING NIGHT!
AND IN FRONT OF PRESS! HOPEFULLY THE TOUR WILL GET SOME GOOD COVERAGE...
SOMETHING'S WRONG...
THE BEAT IS OFF...

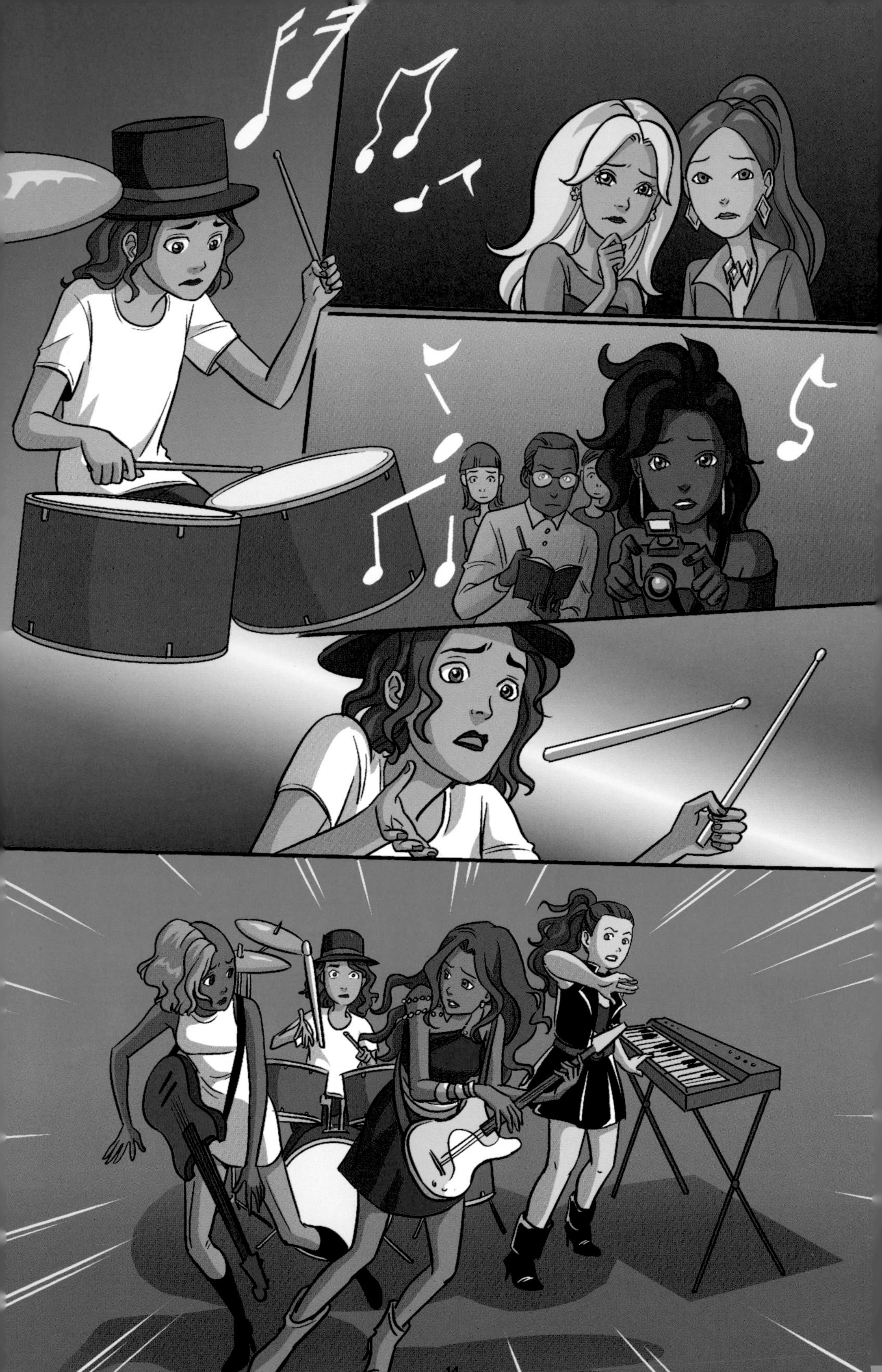

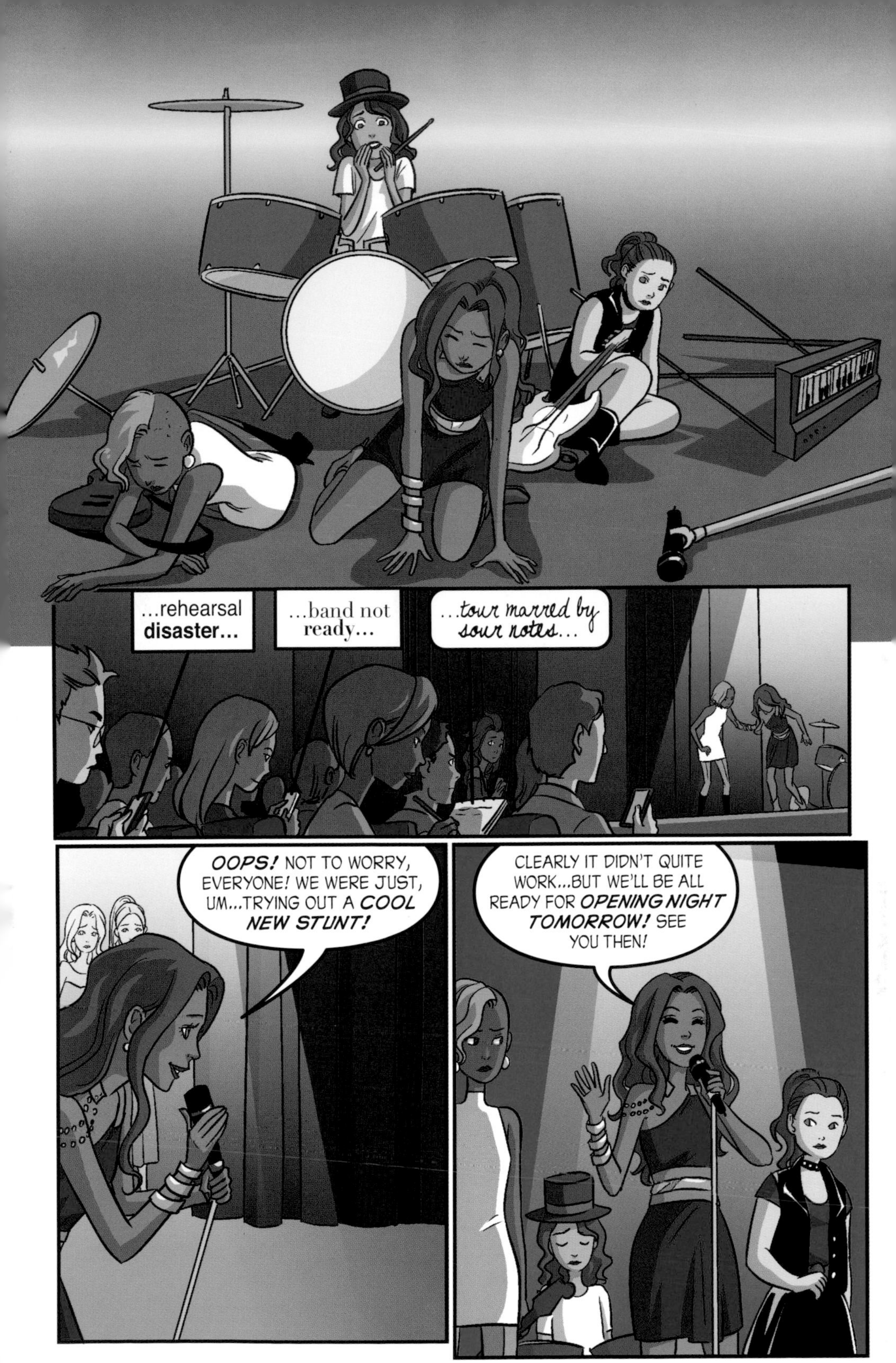
...rehearsal disaster...
...band not ready...
...tour marred by sour notes...
OOPS! NOT TO WORRY, EVERYONE! WE WERE JUST, UM...TRYING OUT A COOL NEW STUNT!
CLEARLY IT DIDN'T QUITE WORK...BUT WE'LL BE ALL READY FOR OPENING NIGHT TOMORROW! SEE YOU THEN!

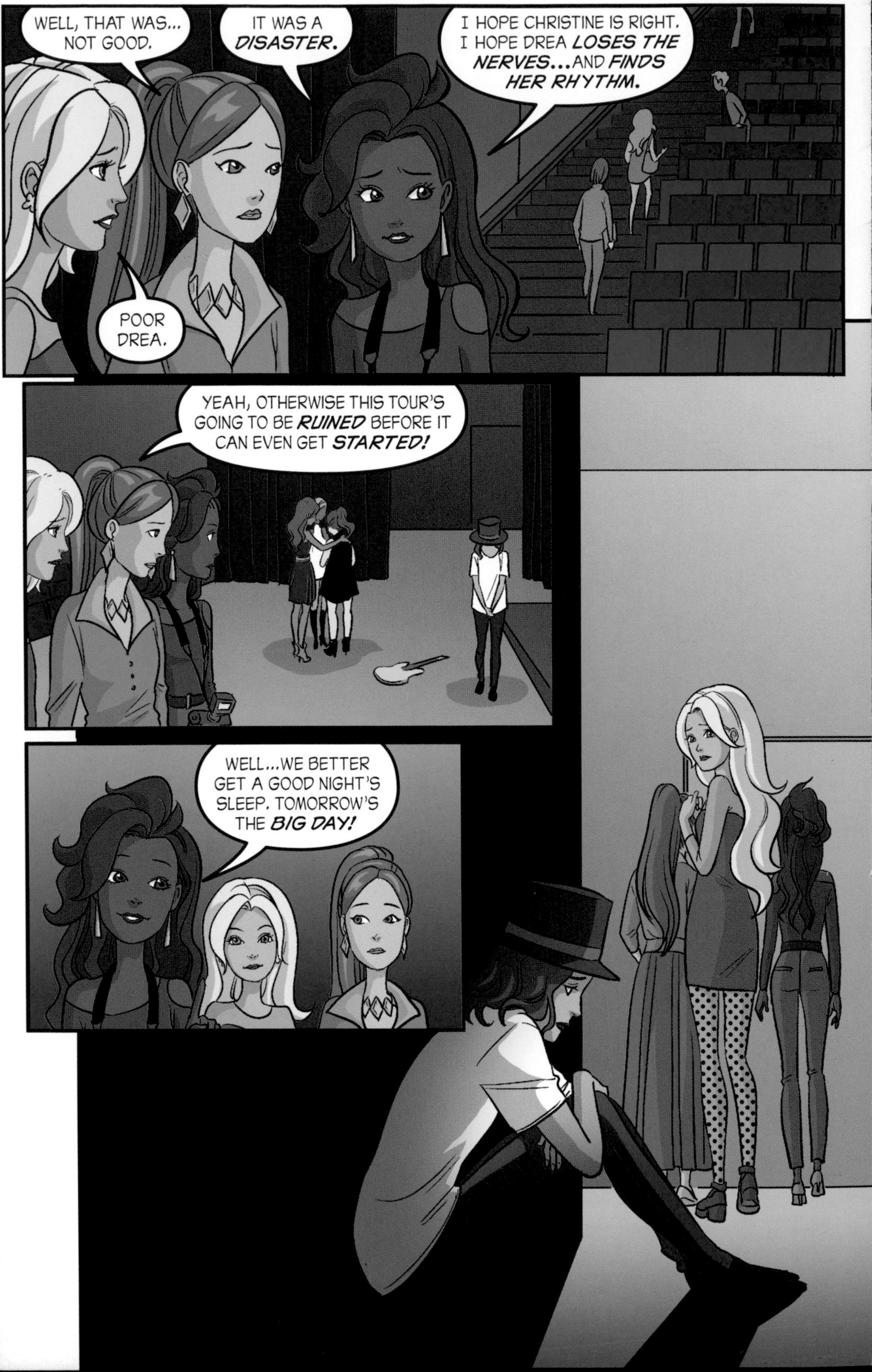
WELL, THAT WAS... NOT GOOD.
IT WAS A DISASTER.
I HOPE CHRISTINE IS RIGHT. I HOPE DREA LOSES THE NERVES...AND FINDS HER RHYTHM.
POOR DREA.
YEAH, OTHERWISE THIS TOUR'S GOING TO BE RUINED BEFORE IT CAN EVEN GET STARTED!
WELL...WE BETTER GET A GOOD NIGHT'S SLEEP. TOMORROW'S THE BIG DAY!

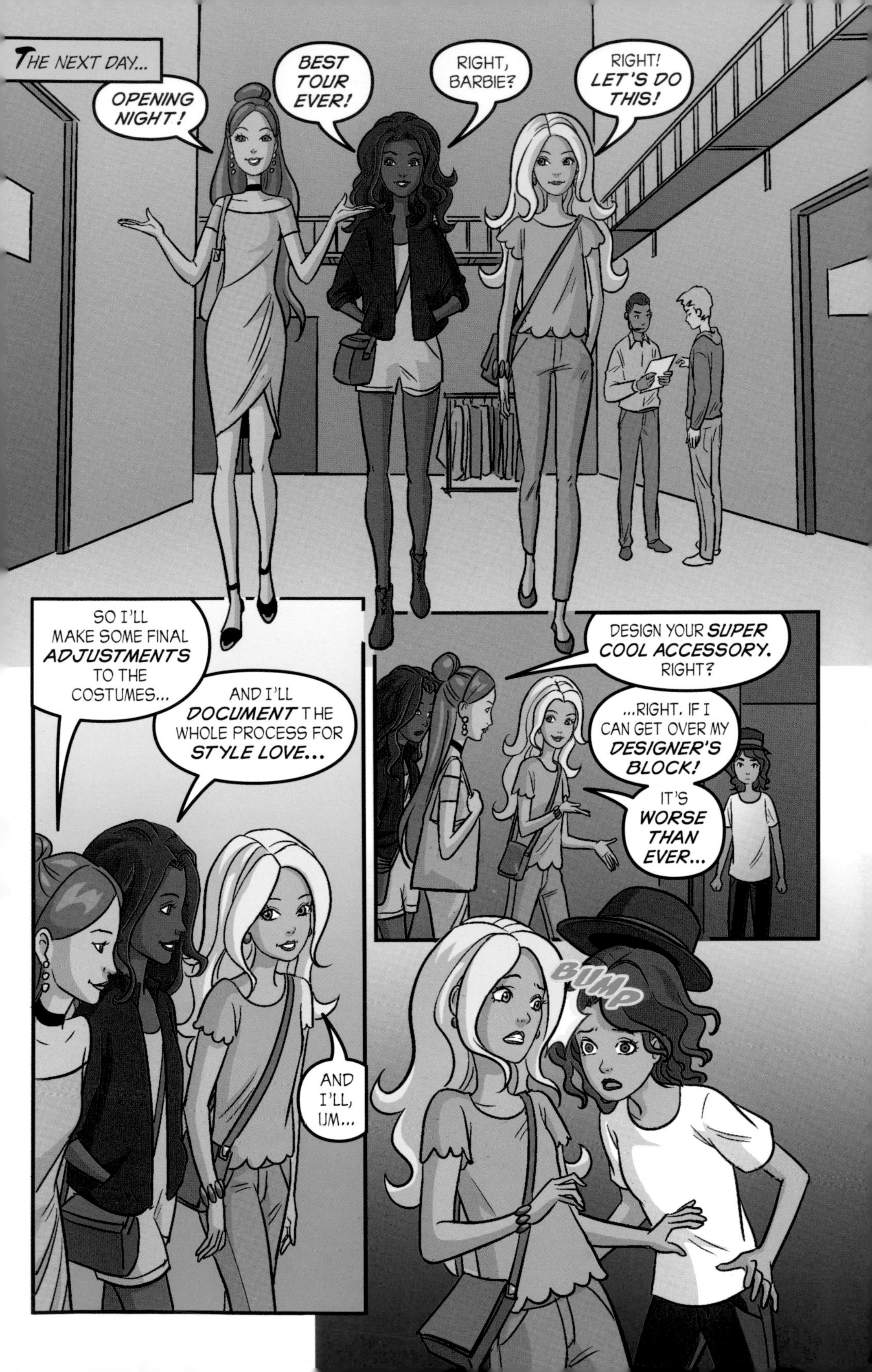
THE NEXT DAY...
OPENING NIGHT!
BEST TOUR EVER!
RIGHT, BARBIE?
RIGHT! LET'S DO THIS!
SO I'LL MAKE SOME FINAL ADJUSTMENTS TO THE COSTUMES...
AND I'LL DOCUMENT THE WHOLE PROCESS FOR STYLE LOVE...
AND I'LL, UM...
DESIGN YOUR SUPER COOL ACCESSORY. RIGHT?
...RIGHT. IF I CAN GET OVER MY DESIGNER'S BLOCK!
IT'S WORSE THAN EVER...
BUMP

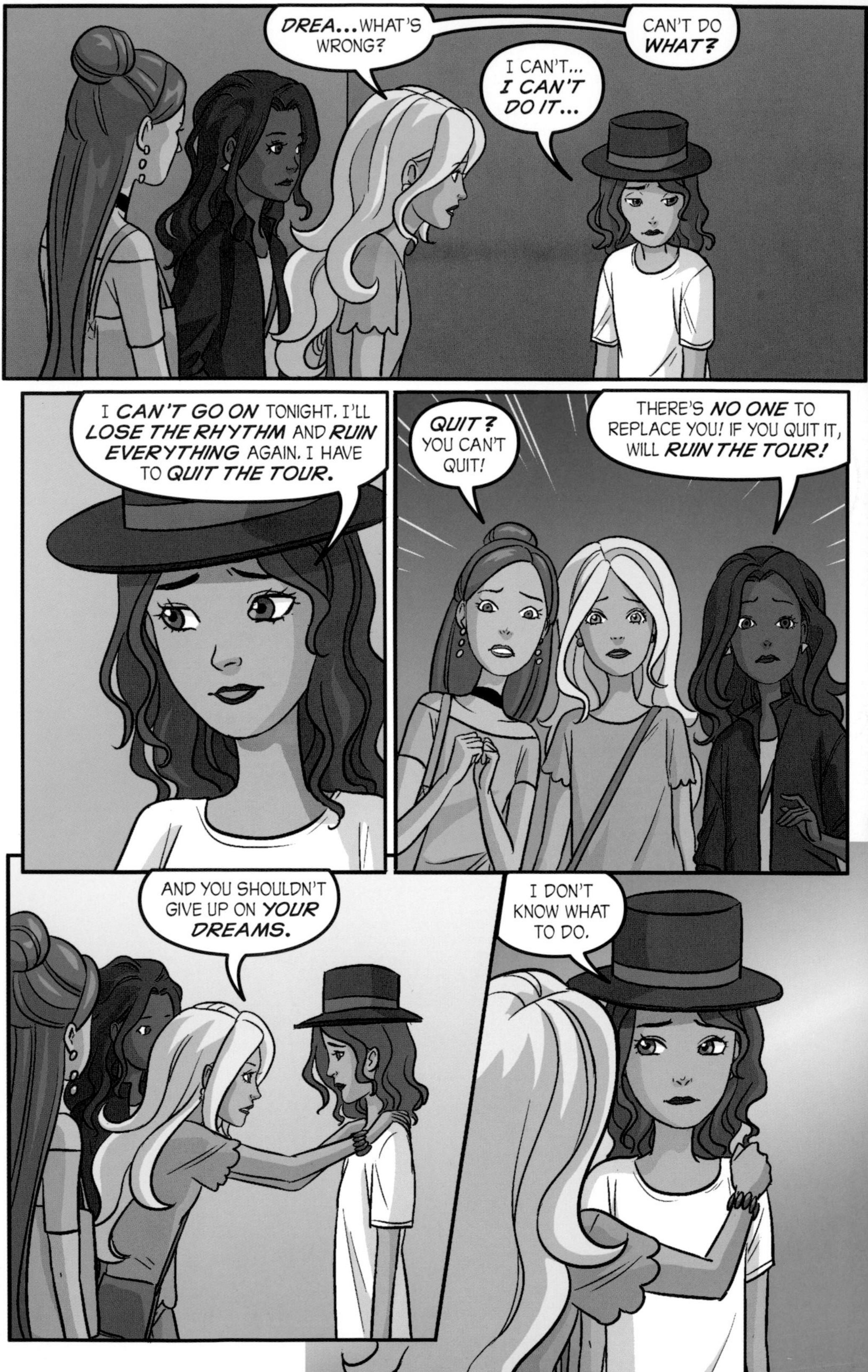
DREA...WHAT'S WRONG?
I CAN'T... I CAN'T DO IT...
CAN'T DO WHAT?
I CAN'T GO ON TONIGHT. I'LL LOSE THE RHYTHM AND RUIN EVERYTHING AGAIN. I HAVE TO QUIT THE TOUR.
QUIT? YOU CAN'T QUIT!
THERE'S NO ONE TO REPLACE YOU! IF YOU QUIT IT, WILL RUIN THE TOUR!
AND YOU SHOULDN'T GIVE UP ON YOUR DREAMS.
I DON'T KNOW WHAT TO DO.

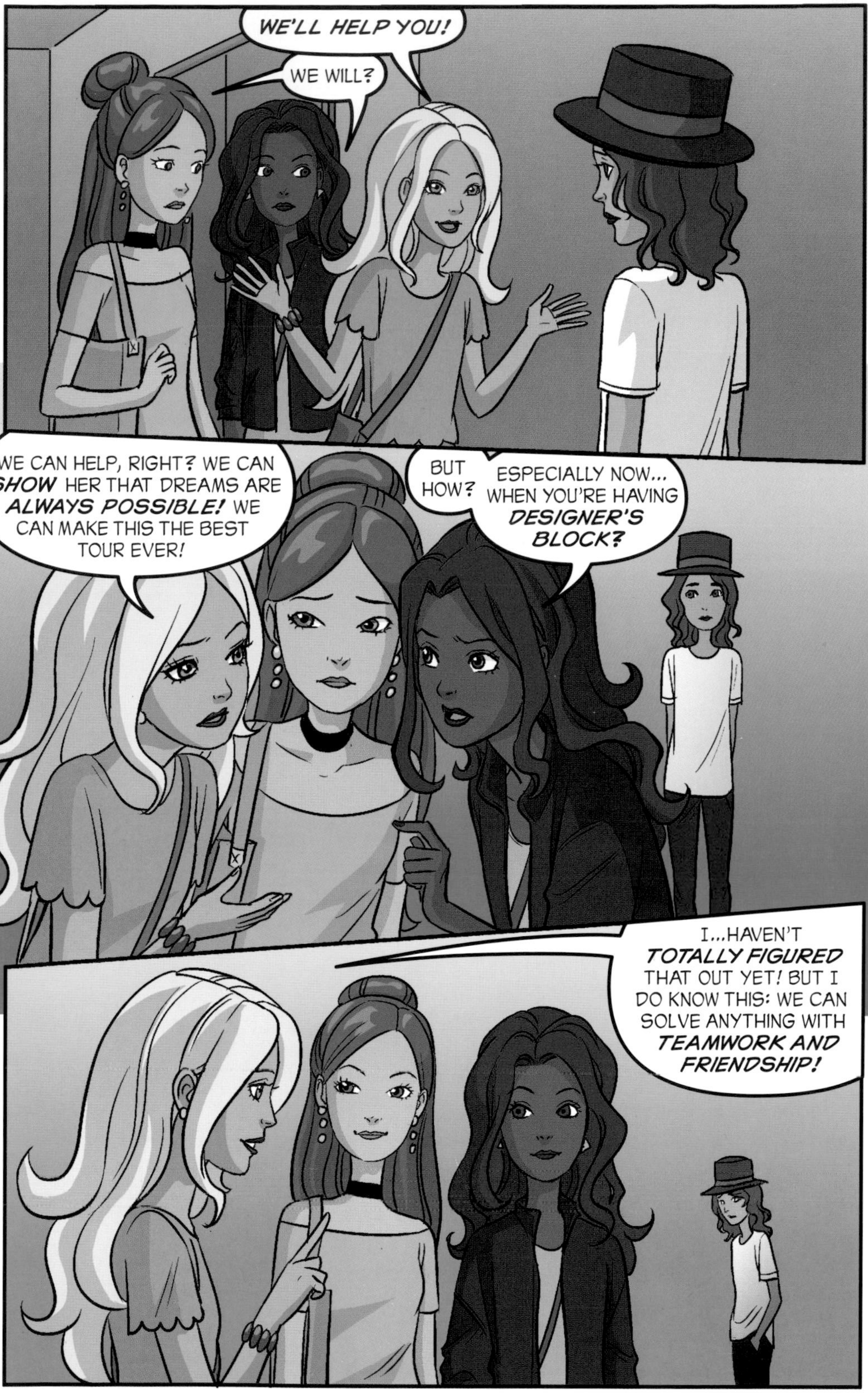

WE'LL HELP YOU!
WE WILL?
WE CAN HELP, RIGHT? WE CAN SHOW HER THAT DREAMS ARE ALWAYS POSSIBLE! WE CAN MAKE THIS THE BEST TOUR EVER!
BUT HOW?
ESPECIALLY NOW... WHEN YOU'RE HAVING DESIGNER'S BLOCK?
I...HAVEN'T TOTALLY FIGURED THAT OUT YET! BUT I DO KNOW THIS: WE CAN SOLVE ANYTHING WITH TEAMWORK AND FRIENDSHIP!

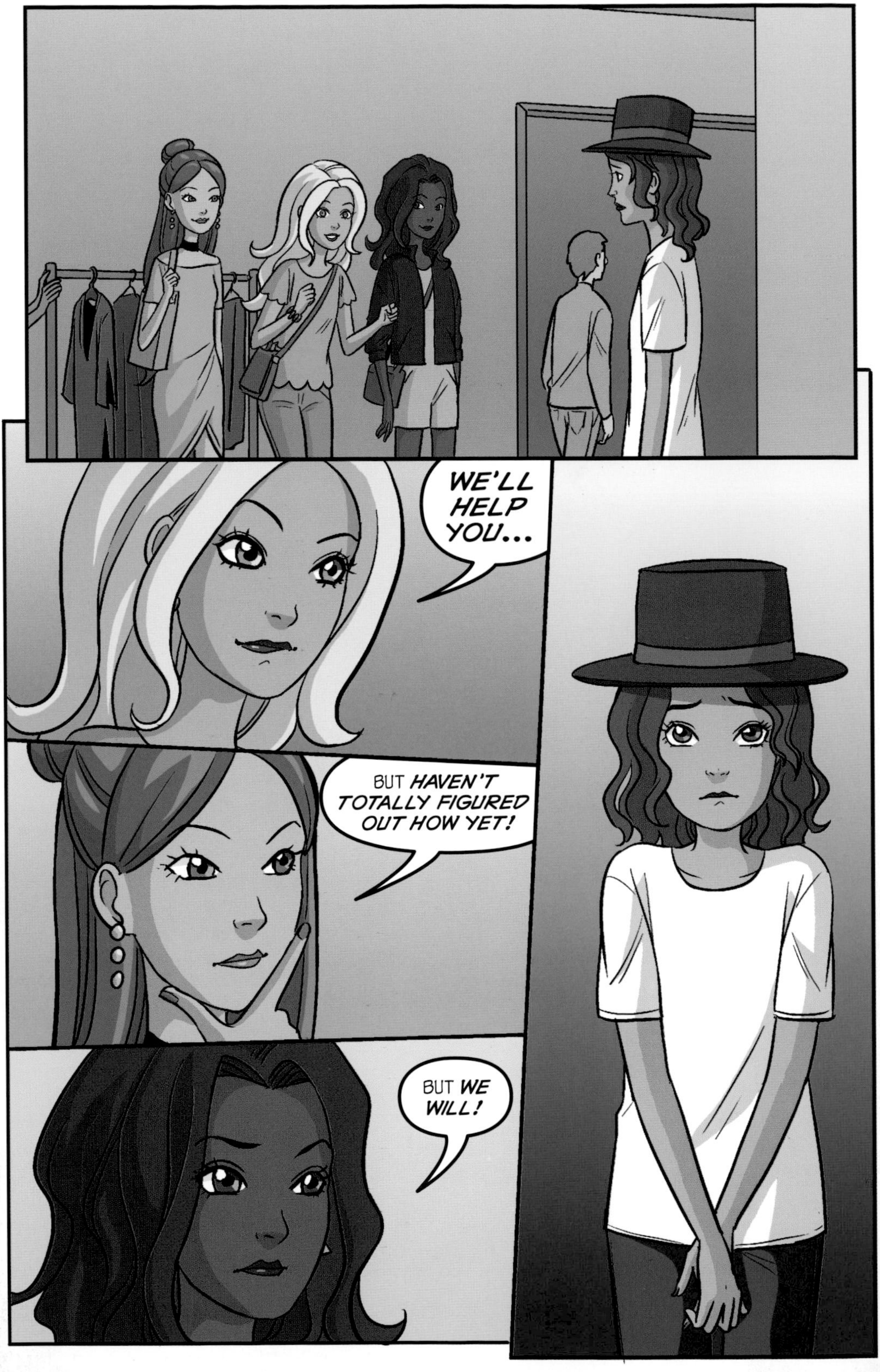
WE'LL HELP YOU...
BUT HAVEN'T TOTALLY FIGURED OUT HOW YET!
BUT WE WILL!

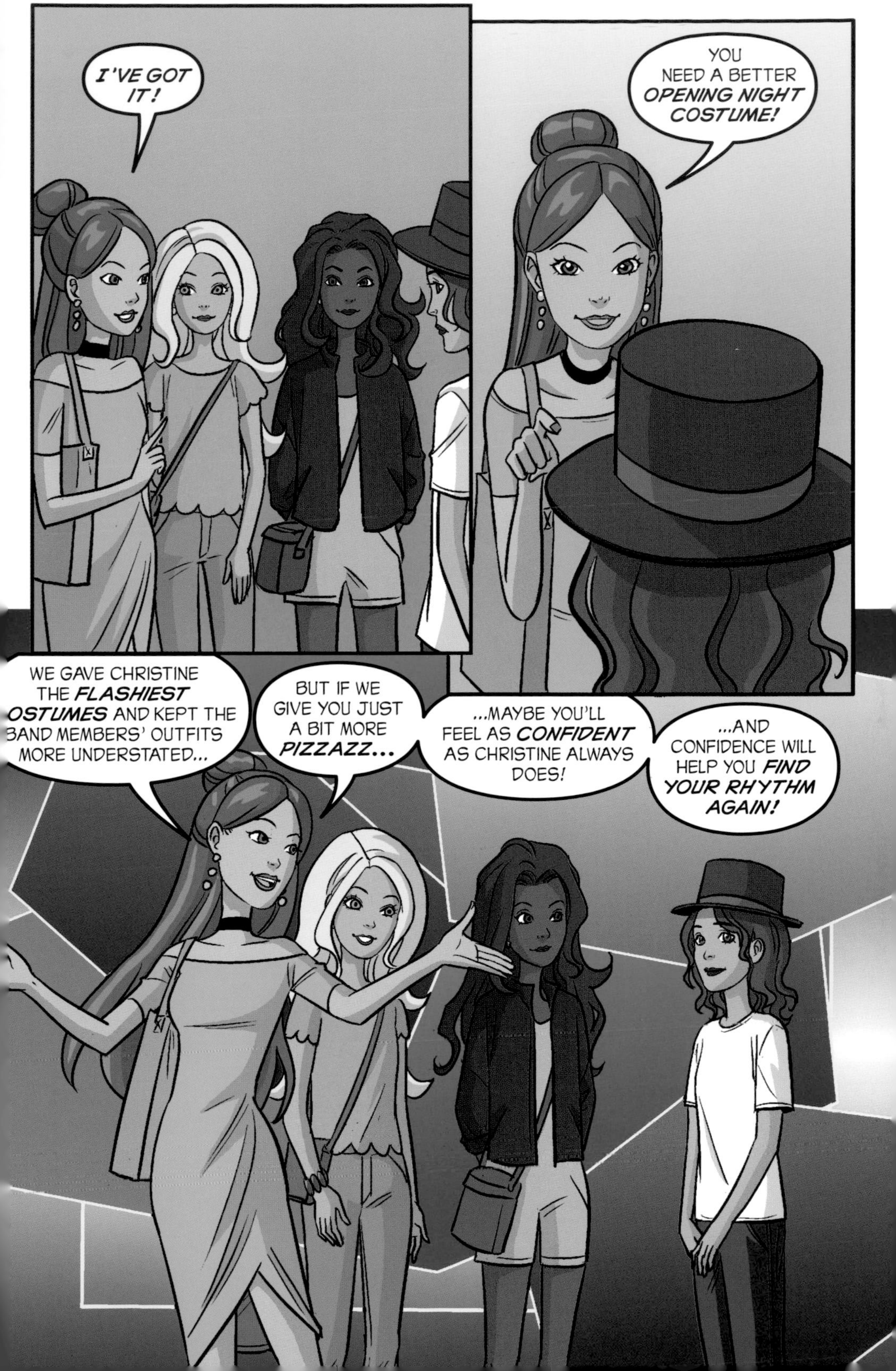

I'VE GOT IT!
YOU NEED A BETTER OPENING NIGHT COSTUME!
WE GAVE CHRISTINE THE FLASHIEST OSTUMES AND KEPT THE BAND MEMBERS' OUTFITS MORE UNDERSTATED...
BUT IF WE GIVE YOU JUST A BIT MORE PIZZAZZ...
...MAYBE YOU'LL FEEL AS CONFIDENT AS CHRISTINE ALWAYS DOES!
...AND CONFIDENCE WILL HELP YOU FIND YOUR RHYTHM AGAIN!

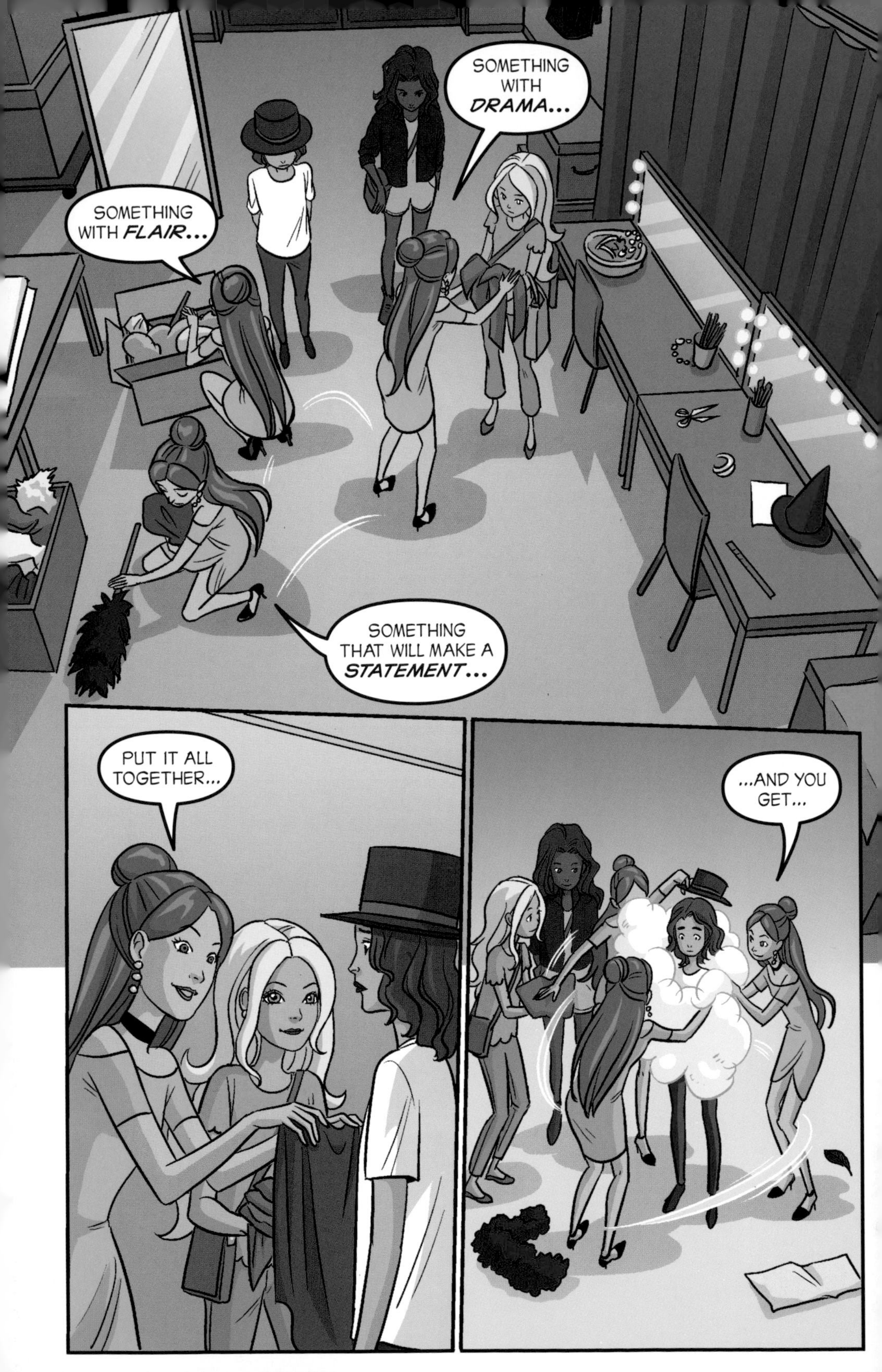
SOMETHING WITH FLAIR...
SOMETHING WITH DRAMA...
SOMETHING THAT WILL MAKE A STATEMENT...
PUT IT ALL TOGETHER...
...AND YOU GET...

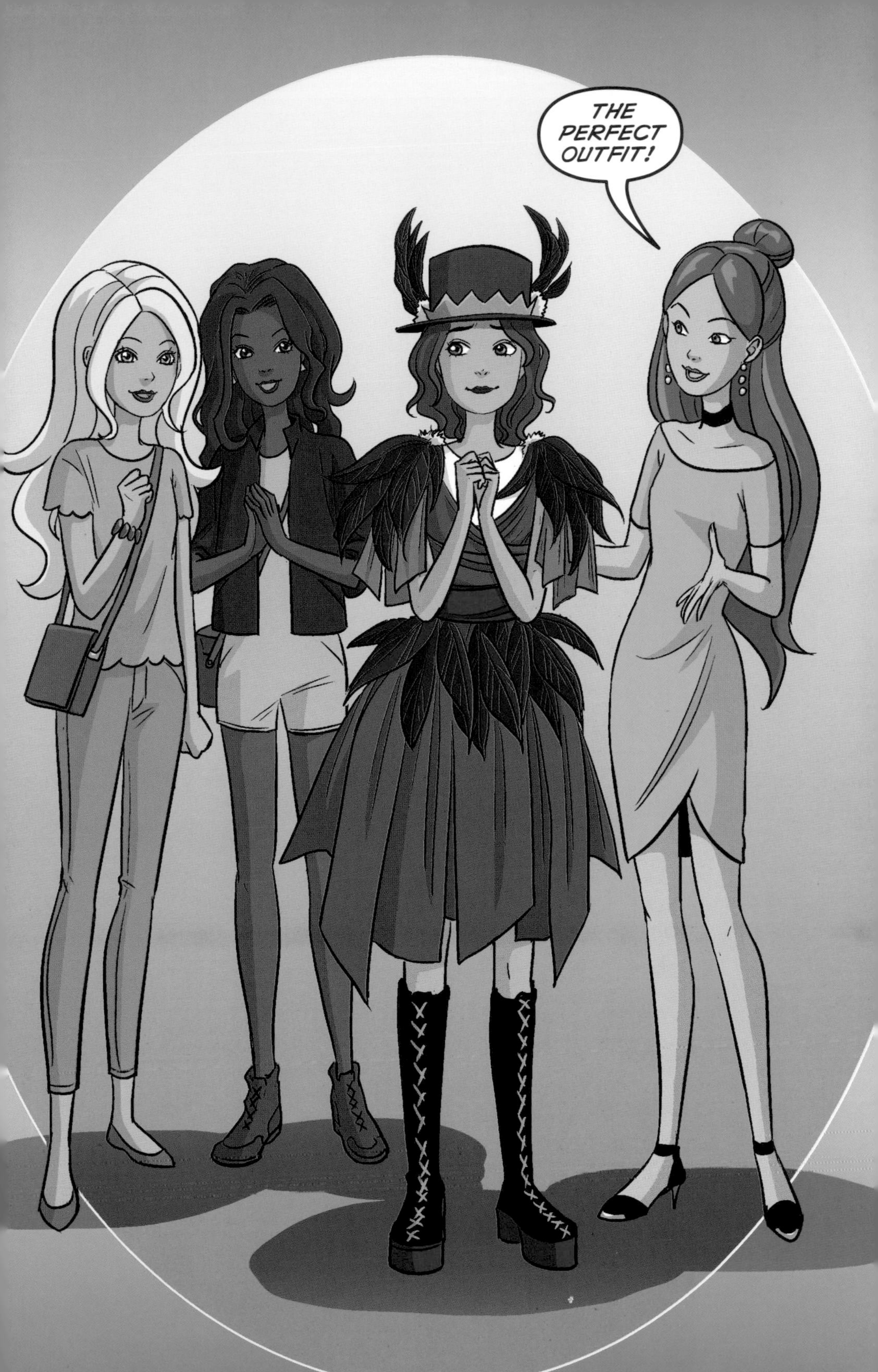
THE PERFECT OUTFIT!

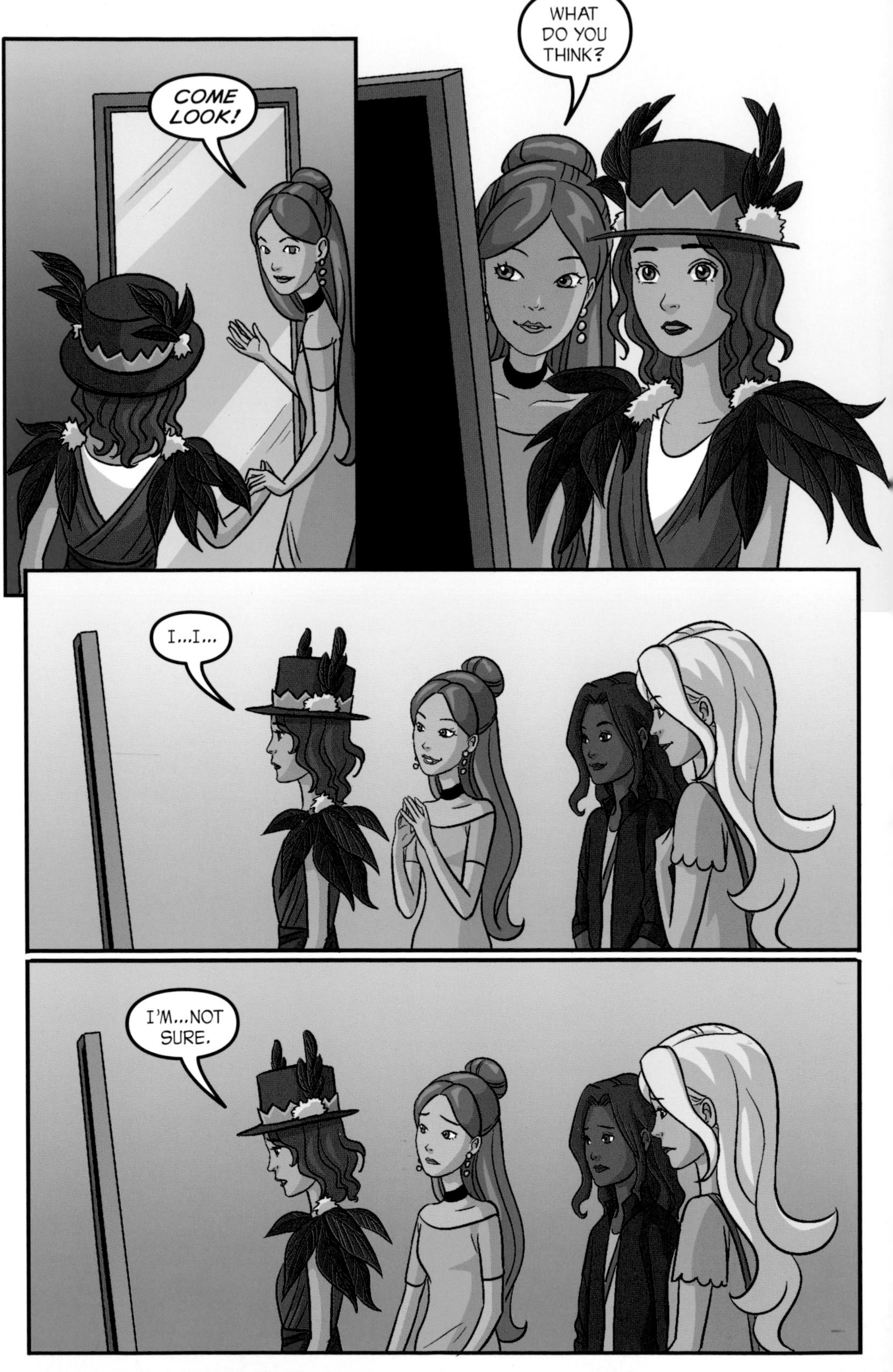
COME LOOK!
WHAT DO YOU THINK?
I...I...
I'M...NOT SURE.

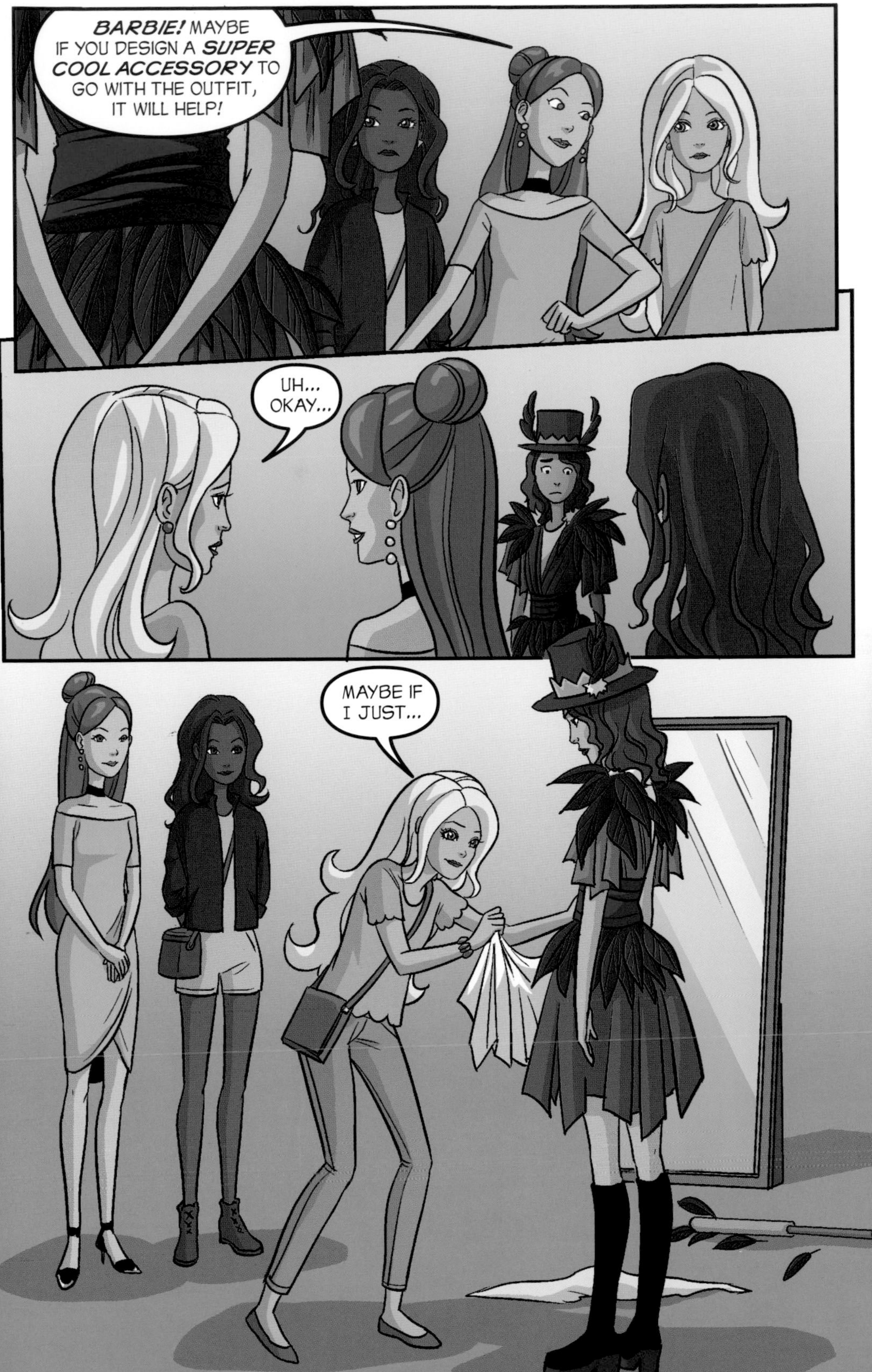
BARBIE! MAYBE IF YOU DESIGN A SUPER COOL ACCESSORY TO GO WITH THE OUTFIT, IT WILL HELP!
UH... OKAY...
MAYBE IF I JUST...

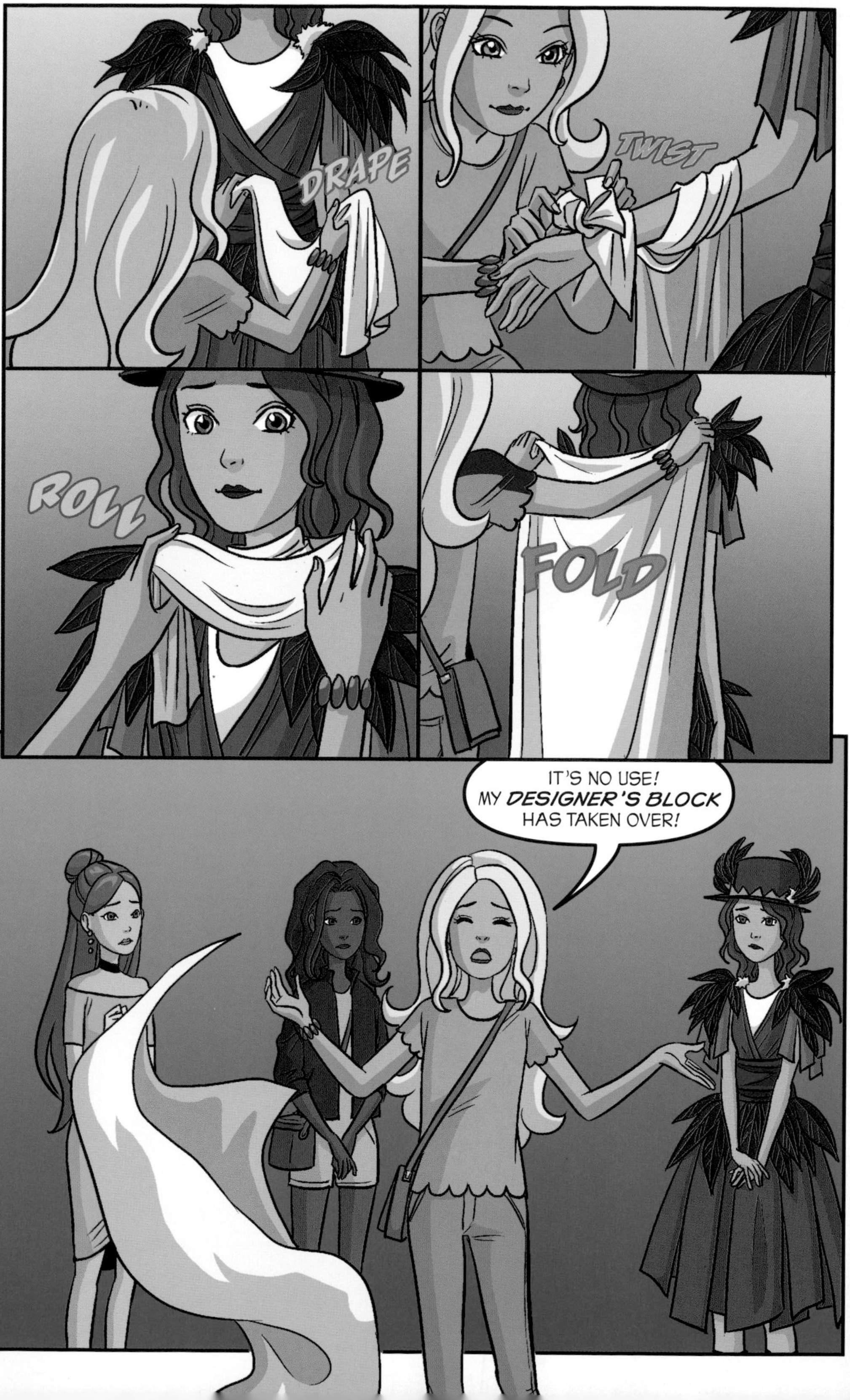
DRAPE
TWIST
ROLL
FOLD
IT'S NO USE! MY DESIGNER'S BLOCK HAS TAKEN OVER!

FLASH
I CAN'T!
FLASH
FLASH
FLASH
FLASH
FLASH
FLASH
FLASH
RIPPPPPPPP
FLASH
FLASH
FLASH
CLIK
CLIK
FLASH
FLASH
CLIK
FLASH

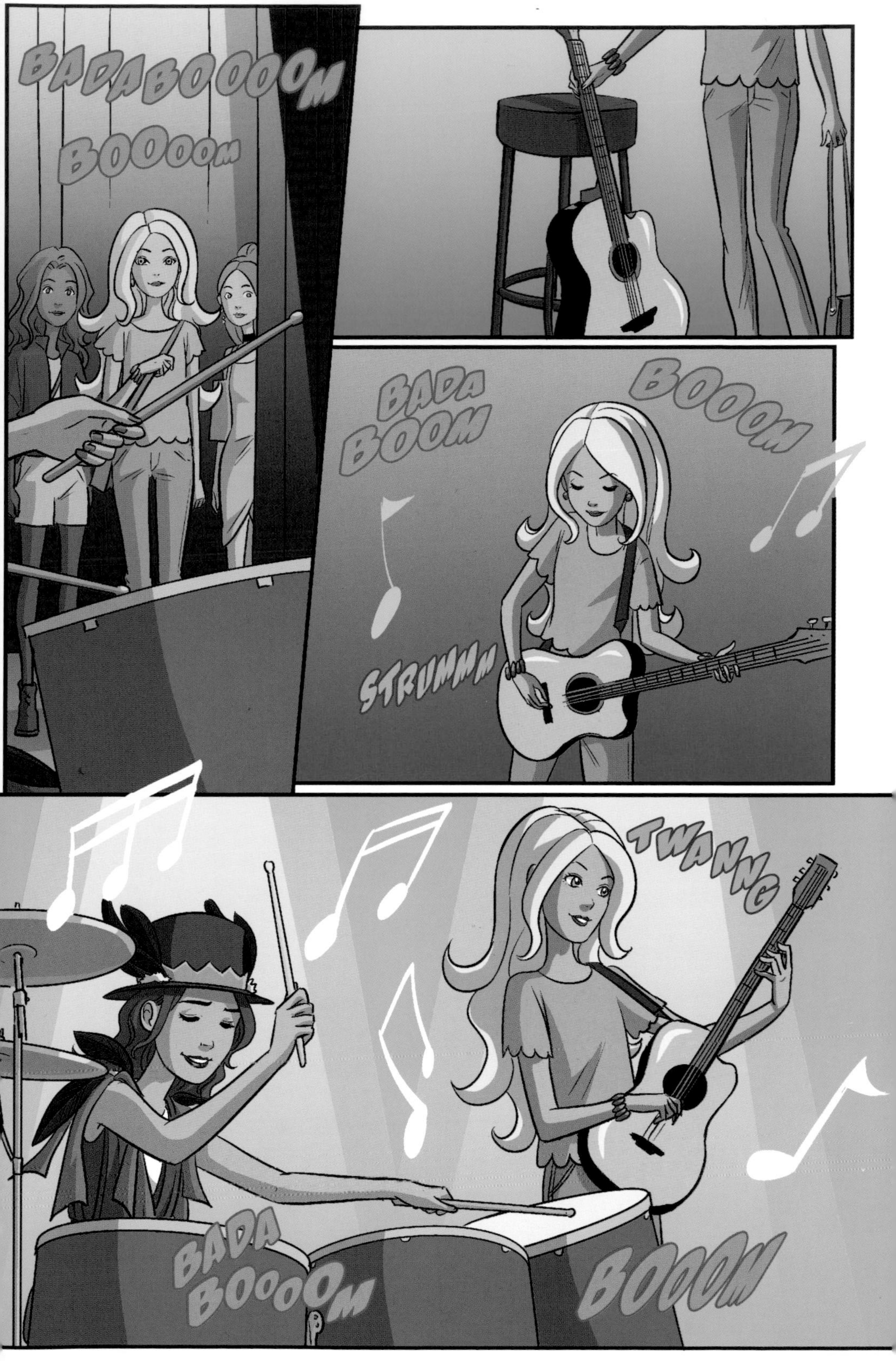
BADABOOOOOM
BOOoom
BADA BOOM
BOOOOM
STRUMMM
TWANNG
BADA BOOOOM
BOOOM

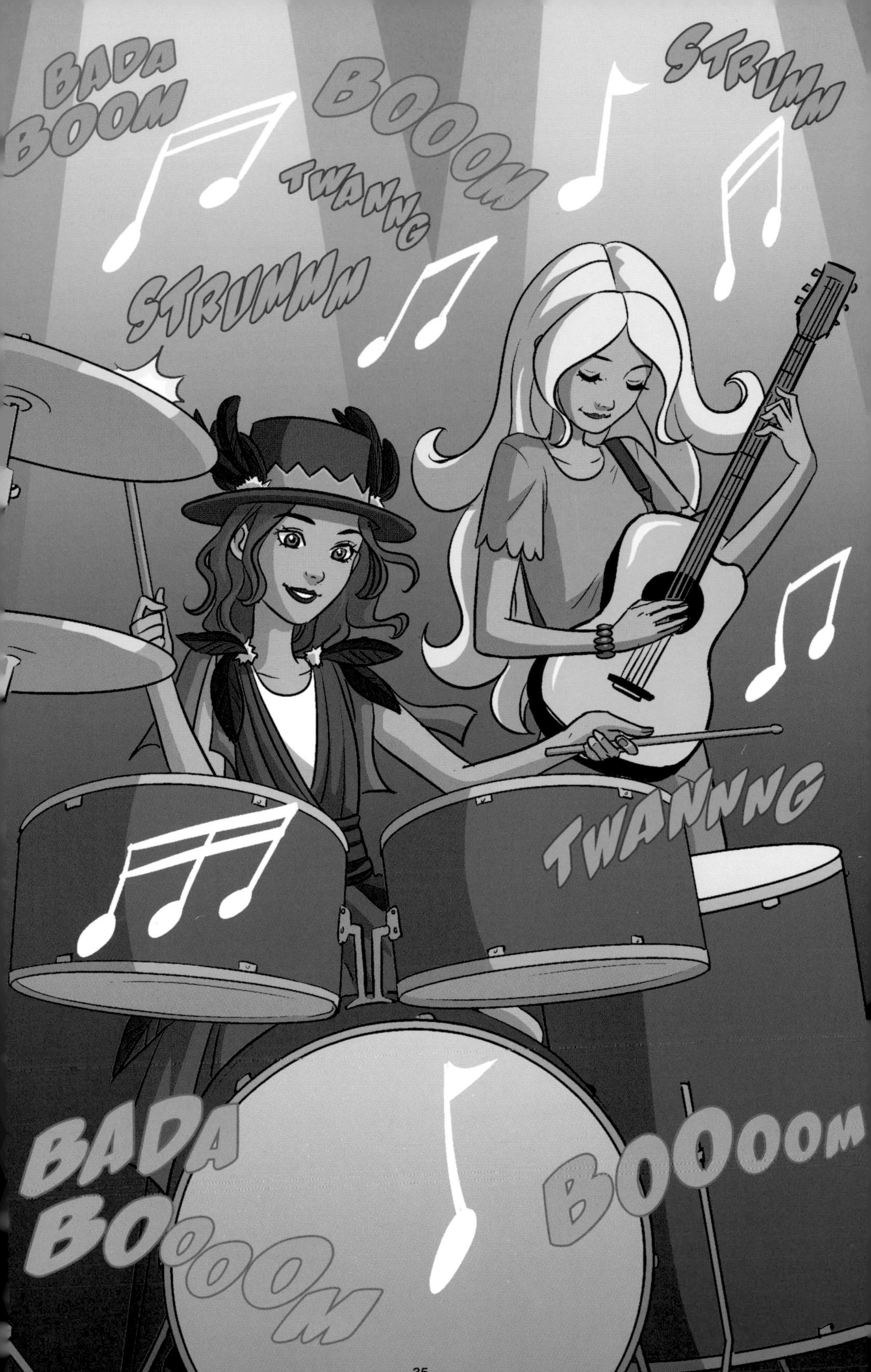
BADA BOOM
BOOOM
TWANNG
STRUMMM
STRUMM
TWANNG
BADA BOOOOM
BOOoom

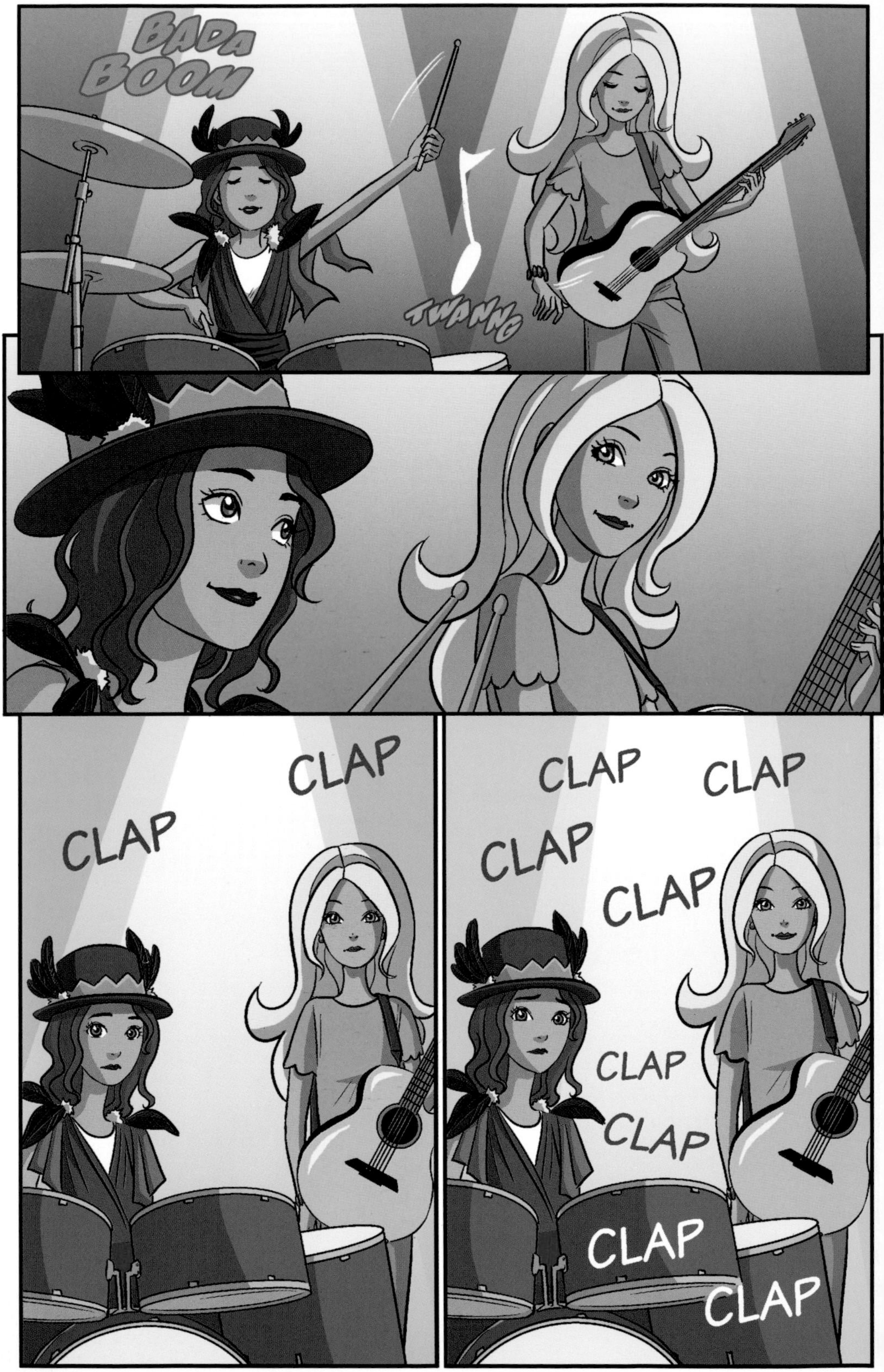
BADA BOOM
TWANNG
CLAP
CLAP
CLAP
CLAP
CLAP
CLAP
CLAP
CLAP
CLAP
CLAP

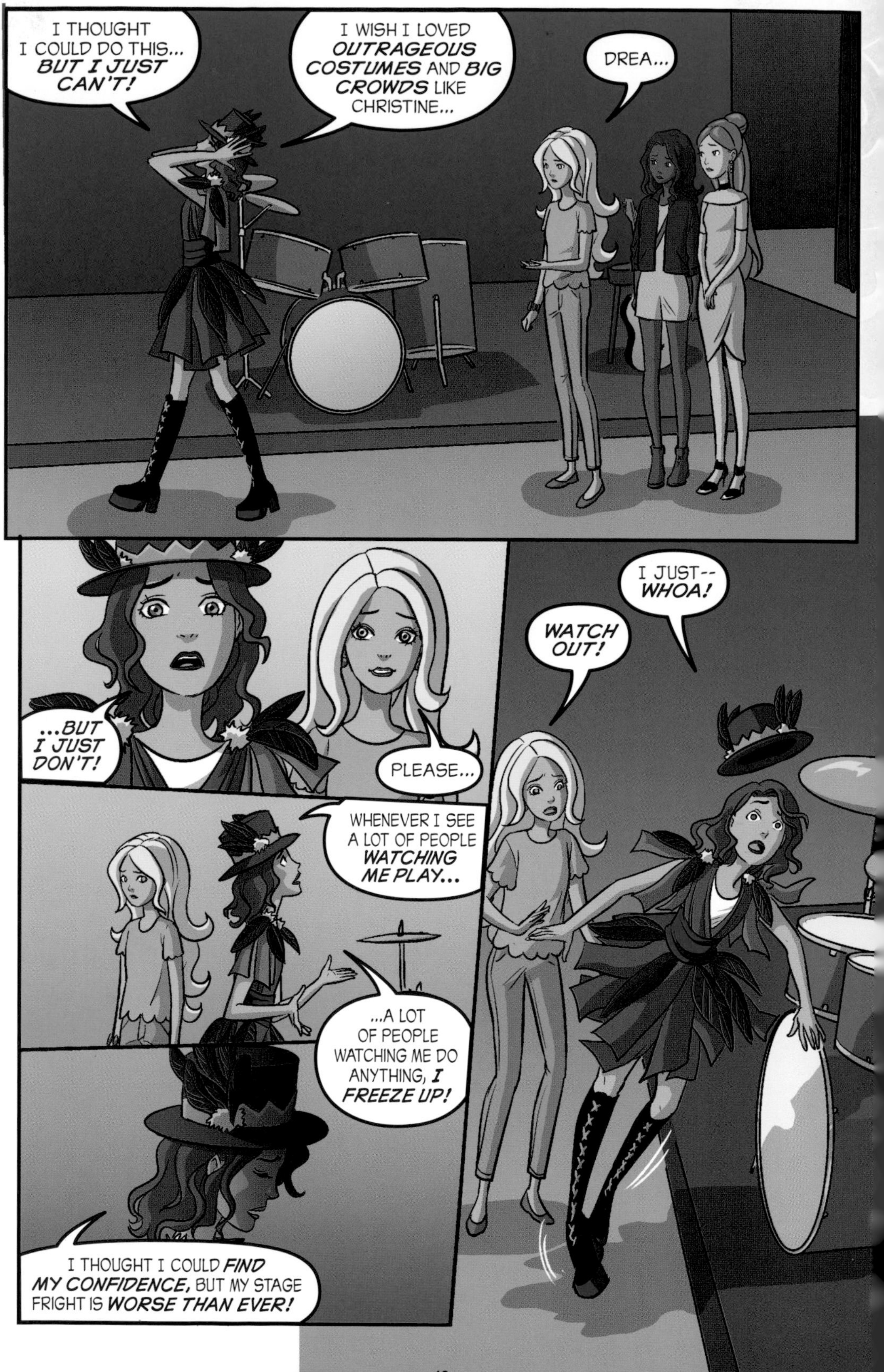

I THOUGHT I COULD DO THIS... BUT I JUST CAN'T!
I WISH I LOVED OUTRAGEOUS COSTUMES AND BIG CROWDS LIKE CHRISTINE...
DREA...
...BUT I JUST DON'T!
PLEASE...
WHENEVER I SEE A LOT OF PEOPLE WATCHING ME PLAY...
...A LOT OF PEOPLE WATCHING ME DO ANYTHING, I FREEZE UP!
I THOUGHT I COULD FIND MY CONFIDENCE, BUT MY STAGE FRIGHT IS WORSE THAN EVER!
I JUST-- WHOA!
WATCH OUT!

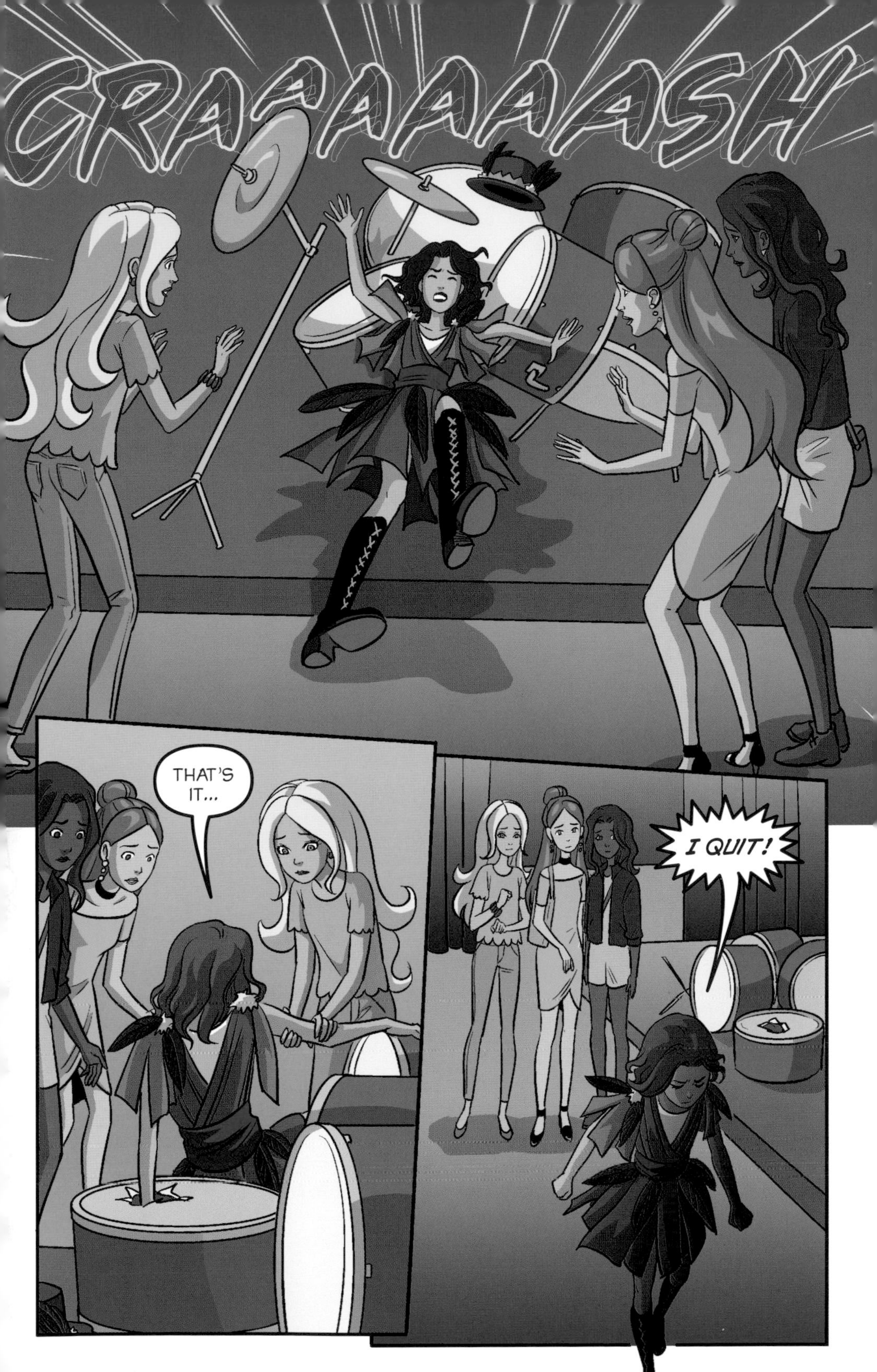
CRAAAAAASH
THAT'S IT...
I QUIT!

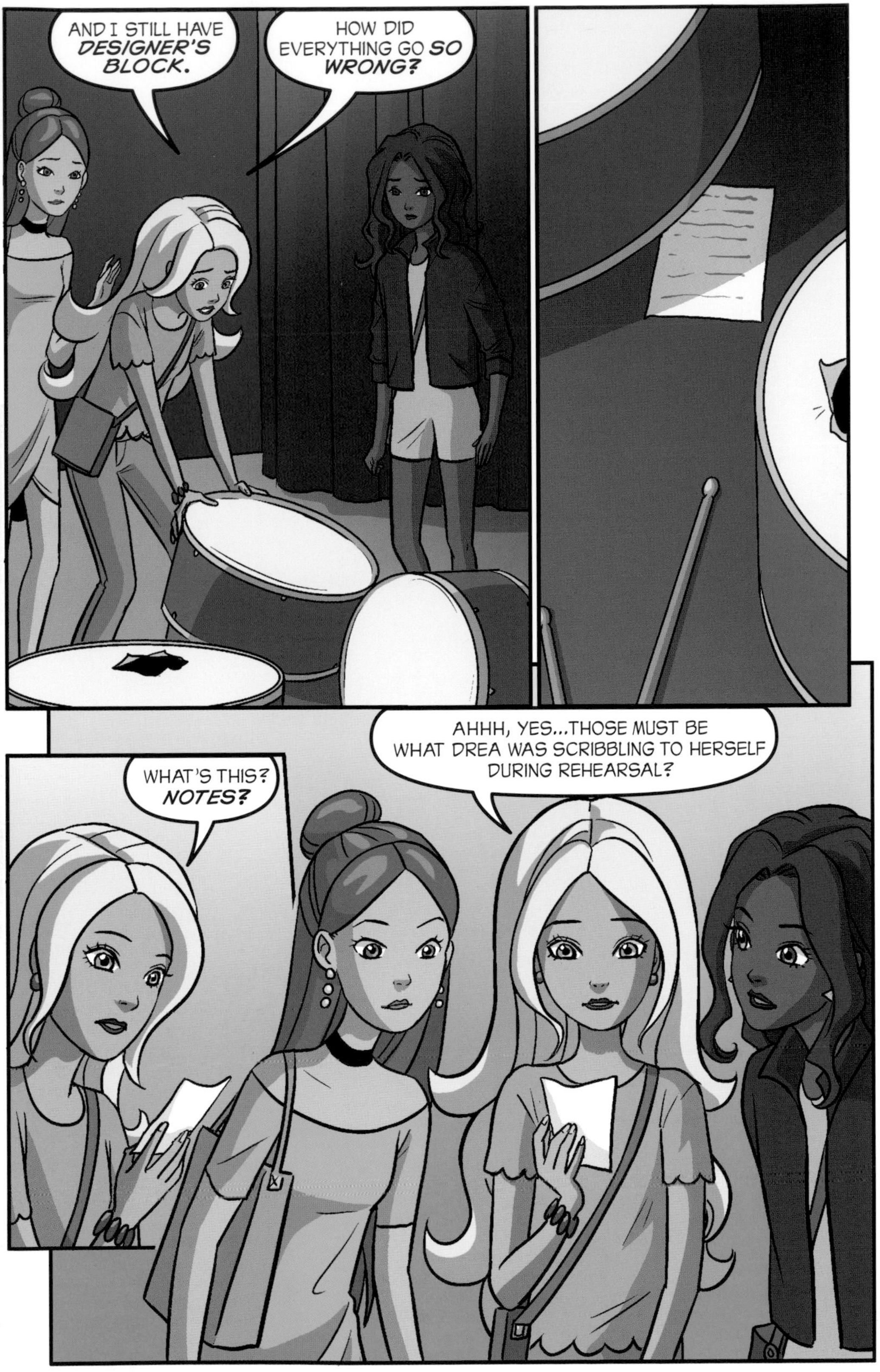
AND I STILL HAVE *DESIGNER'S BLOCK.*
HOW DID EVERYTHING GO *SO WRONG?*
WHAT'S THIS? *NOTES?*
AHHH, YES...THOSE MUST BE WHAT DREA WAS SCRIBBLING TO HERSELF DURING REHEARSAL?

I THINK I SHOULD TRY TALKING TO HER *MYSELF.*

GO FOR IT.

GOOD LUCK.

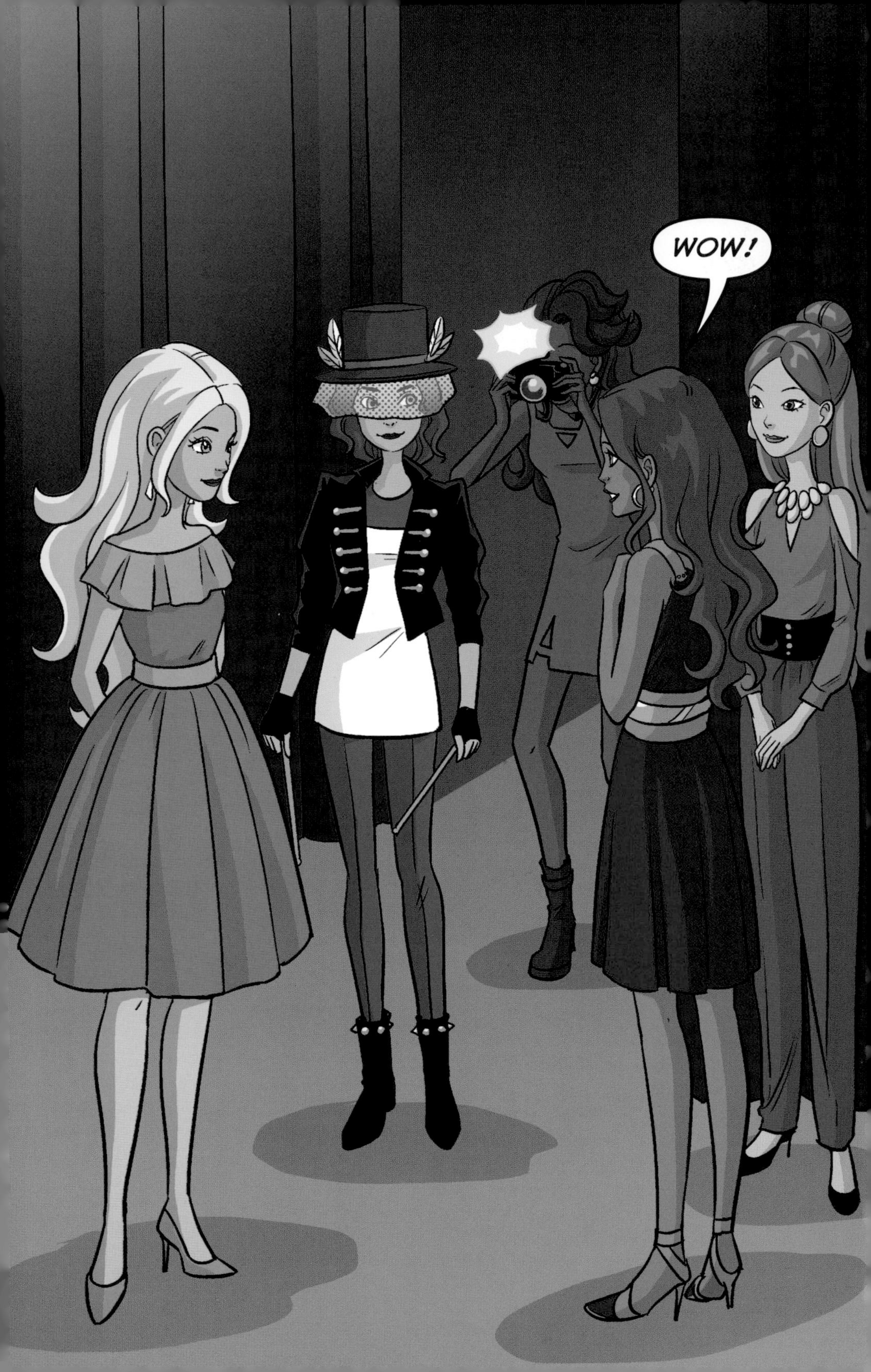
WOW!

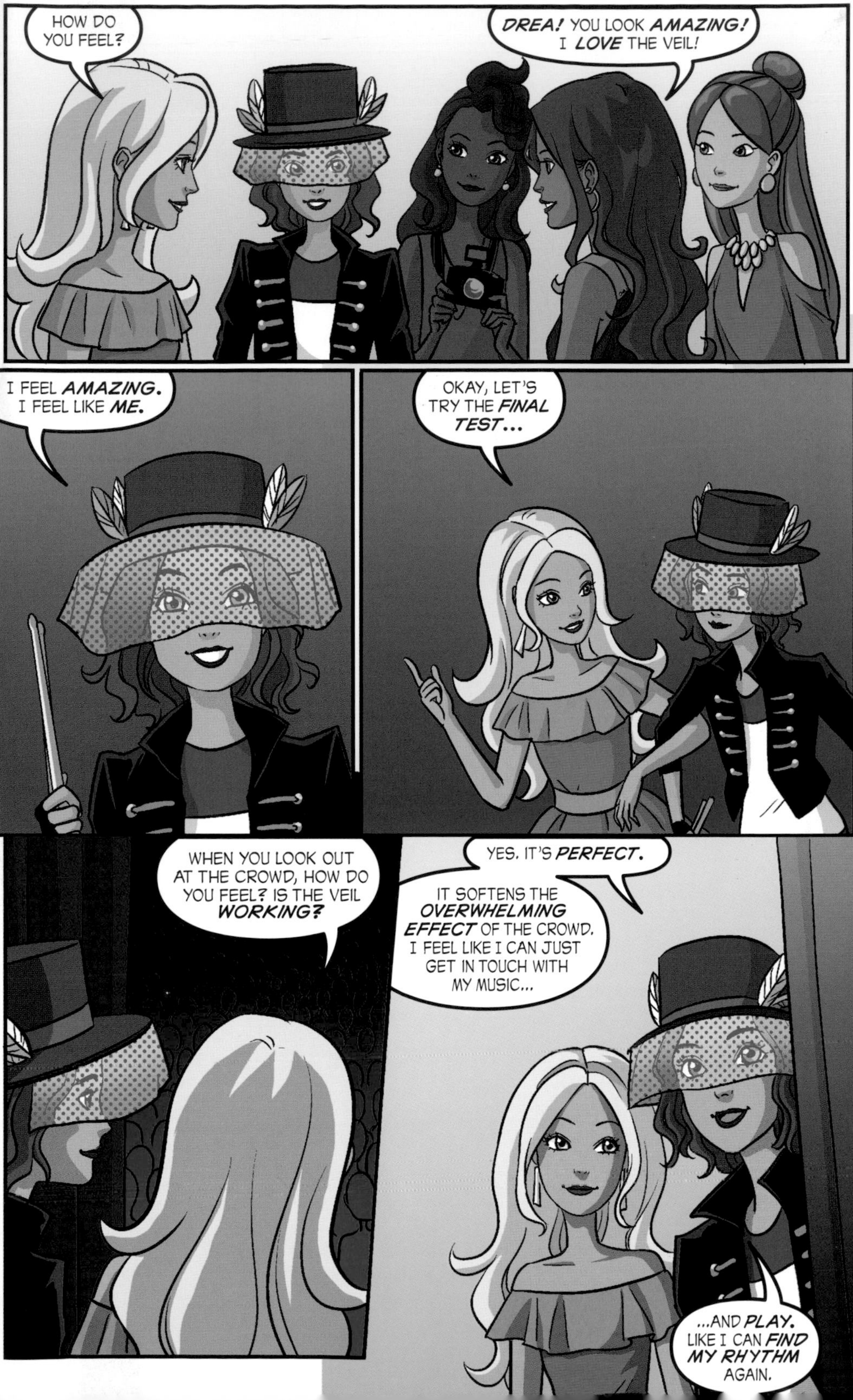
HOW DO YOU FEEL?
DREA! YOU LOOK AMAZING! I LOVE THE VEIL!
I FEEL AMAZING. I FEEL LIKE ME.
OKAY, LET'S TRY THE FINAL TEST...
WHEN YOU LOOK OUT AT THE CROWD, HOW DO YOU FEEL? IS THE VEIL WORKING?
YES. IT'S PERFECT.
IT SOFTENS THE OVERWHELMING EFFECT OF THE CROWD. I FEEL LIKE I CAN JUST GET IN TOUCH WITH MY MUSIC...
...AND PLAY. LIKE I CAN FIND MY RHYTHM AGAIN.

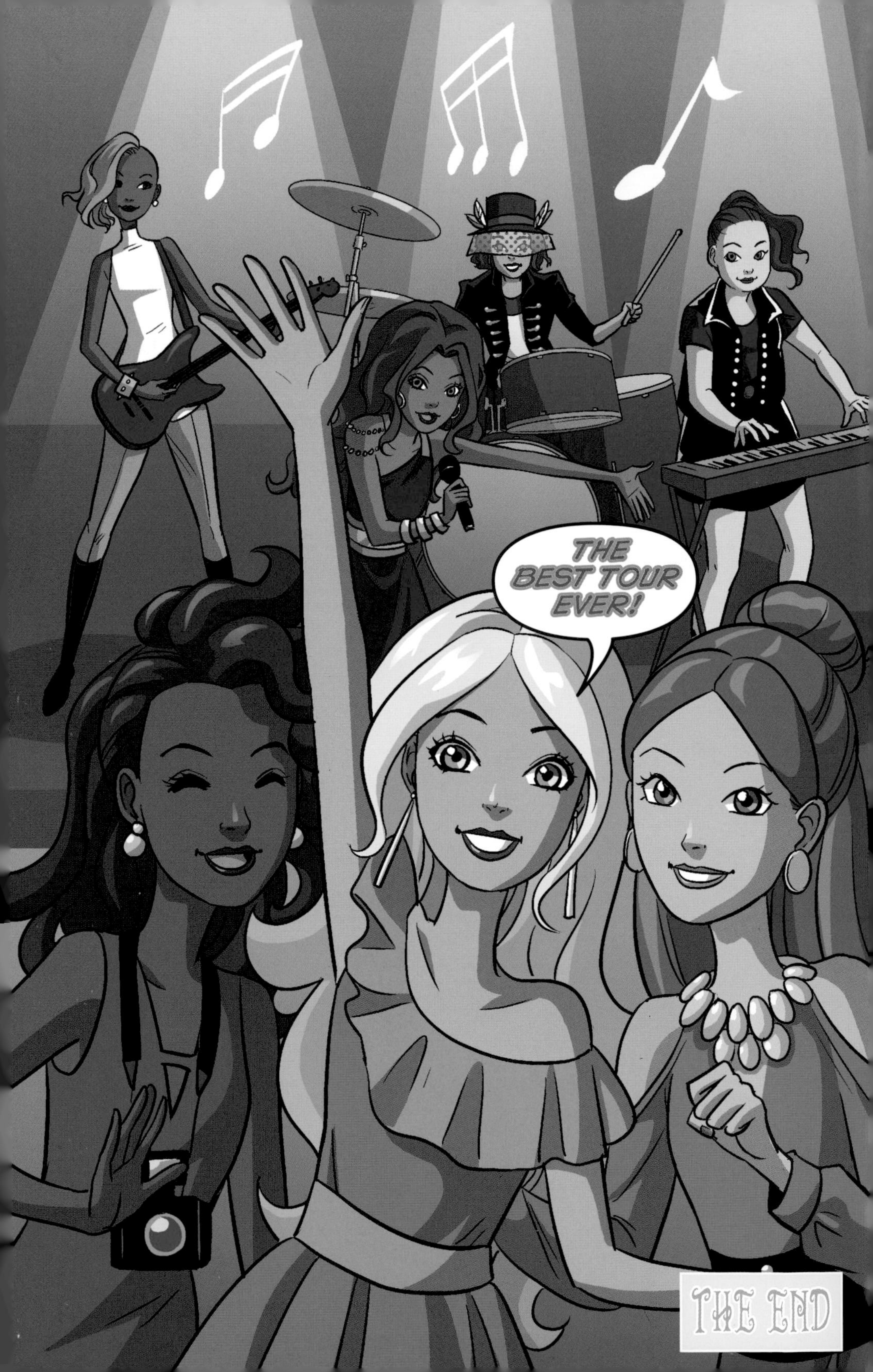
THE BEST TOUR EVER!
THE END